Mary Hartwell Catherwood

The Dogberry Bunch

Mary Hartwell Catherwood

The Dogberry Bunch

ISBN/EAN: 9783337417826

Printed in Europe, USA, Canada, Australia, Japan

Cover: Foto ©Andreas Hilbeck / pixelio.de

More available books at **www.hansebooks.com**

THE DOGBERRY BUNCH.

BY

MARY HARTWELL CATHERWOOD.

BOSTON
D LOTHROP COMPANY
FRANKLIN AND HAWLEY STREETS

CONTENTS.

———◆———

(v.)

THE DOGBERRY BUNCH.

CHAPTER I.

THE 'SOCIATION.

N the state of Illinois there was a two-sided village ; in that village there was a small frame dwelling ; in that dwelling a large square table ; and around this table sat the Dogberry Bunch. Like the family of Wordsworth's little cotter, they were seven in all. Seven live and unlike but strongly-united brothers and sisters, without father or mother to take care of them or sit with them at table. Their parents had been dead more than a year ; and as they got on very comfortably as they were, and their guardian did not know what else to do with them, he let them alone.

Alice at the head of the table, and Ben at the foot, were the recognized Heads of the House. Alice was eighteen — more than a year older than he — but her plump figure scarcely reached to his shoulder. Being Miss Dogberry, and of age, she had come into her estate which consisted in plans to get along, and working as assistant teacher in the schools to help the Bunch. They owned nothing but this house situated among shady trees, and an adjoining lot used for a garden, which their well-wishers prophesied would sell for a pretty price by and by. I could not enumerate the sad and hard-working years which the elder Dogberrys spent in saving even this inheritance for their children, out of sickness and hardship. But with the little house they left their Bunch a feeling of true independence. Accustomed to work and to obey their elders, they now worked on, obedient to what they had been taught. Ben, a large fine boy, with a ruddy face and deep-set eyes, was learning to be a carpenter. Jack, ugly but charming, and full of resources, was messenger-boy in the railroad depot and general gardener and repairer at home. Lucy was house-keeper and Maude her assistant. Rheem, when he and this latter and favorite sister were not

at school, found "jobs" to do which enriched him
and helped him maintain an honorable place in the
Bunch's Association. Arthur, the milk white, big-
browed, three-year-old baby, was the only one of the
family who had not stated duties.

Around this square table I mentioned, the Bunch
were disposed according to their likes. Although a
firm Bunch, they hung in twos. Maude, colorless,
with long fair hair and black-lashed eyes, of course
sat close by her twin, Rheem, who had more color
and more size; they answered to the names of
Rome and Remus. Ben and Alice were "Ben Bolt"
and "Sweet Alice;" and Jack and Arthur were uneven
sized mates. Lucy alone went companionless; but

"SWEET ALICE."

as she was the house-
mother they all be-
longed to her; be-
sides she was so tall
the Bunch said she
would do for two any-
way. She was indeed
the young giraffe of
the flock, Benjamin
being obliged to
stretch after his inches
to keep her down.

They ate their supper with great relish : it was a

comfortable supper of bread and milk, apple-sauce and gingerbread, and, the season being early June, a heaping saucer of strawberries flanked each young Dogberry's plate, from the strawberry vines in their garden.

"Wouldn't it be nice," exclaimed Jack, who appropriately first breaks silence in this history, being the tinkler who usually led the flock, "if we'd all do as children do in stories : set out to seek our fortunes ! All start from this house and agree to meet in a year, or several years, and every fellow try to bring back the most ! "

"But who'd keep house while we were gone ? " inquired Maude.

"O, the house could keep itself like it always does ! "

"Romr and Rheem."

"I guess Loo doesn't find that to be the case," remarked Ben, smiling on the housekeeper.

"Jack always thinks the bread makes itself, and his clothes get clean only with his wearing them — "

"O, I'm not denying you're useful, Lucephus," cried gay Jack, "you're good for a well-rope, and you'd make a first-rate step-ladder; and if you only would take your stand in the garden and stay there I'd never have to cut a bean-pole."

"I don't think such remarks sound very well, addressed to your sister," came the soft contralto of Alice the teacher, who far from being the young lady which a city girl at her age would appear, was only a plump, fair child like the others, but with more gravity, and with longer dresses than Lucy's. Country girls mature slowly.

At this instant Rheem started up, exploding the question :

"How much money has the 'Sociation, now, Treasurer?" Upon this, all the seven faces including Arthur's — he always imitating his brothers and sisters — put on a serious look, and the seven voices inquired cautiously as became the voices of stockholders :

"Why?"

"Because, if we've got much as six dollars and a half we can buy the nicest pig of Mr. Smith and fat him for winter!"

"We need a pig," admitted Ben, in meditation.

"The prettiest little fellow," pleaded Rheem;

" and I'll take care of him, and Jack will make a pen if he is as smart as he is at fixing up some other things "—

Here Jack winked pleadingly and shook his head at Remus.

" But isn't it against our rules," said Lucy, " to spend the Association money on things for our use? I thought it was to start a — a — "

" A fund," said Ben.

"Well, Rome is secretary," cried Jack. " Better get the papers and see."

Maude ran accordingly to the candle-box in which her valuables were stored, and returned with a fistfull of paper bits. As she turned these records over, a desire arose from the family to thoroughly review their Association; so at their request she read the following Constitution and By-laws :

THE ASSOCIATION.

We want to Club together to save money because we are orphans and got to look out for ourselves. And we do not want to be separated. Each one must put in what he can, and vote what will be done with it.

BY-LAWS.

1st. None of this money can be drawn out to spend for candy.

2nd. If four of the Association agree to any investment, the rest will have to give up.

3rd. Every month we will take ten cents out of our fund to give to the Lord.

4th. No member can draw the Association money unless all the others are agreed.

6th. It shall be invested in the best ways we can find out.

Signed :

BENJAMIN DOGBERRY,
ALICE DOGBERRY,
JACK DOGBERRY,
LUCY DOGBERRY,
RHEEM DOGBERRY,
MAUDE DOGBERRY,

his
ARTHUR ⋈ DOGBERRY
mark

Maude, Secretary.

"Now, there's nothing said in these documents about pigs," said Jack.

"But there's nothing said against them!" cried Remus warmly.

"It says," repeated Maude in support of her favorite brother, "if four agree to any investment, the rest will have to give up. *You* made that by-law yourself, Mr. Jack!"

" But," objected Alice, "it wouldn't be a real investment to buy something we were going to eat up. We intended the Association to save for us."

"Well, let us vote," suggested Ben, amicably, " I'm president. All in favor of putting the Association money in a pig to fat and kill, hold up the hand ! "

Perhaps this was not a fair way to put the question, and influence the voters. Remus looked aggrieved as he thrust up both hands, that nobody but his twin seconded him.

"Well," resumed the president : "now all in favor of *not* investing in pig, hold up the hand ! "

All the other hands went up, including Arthur's and his milk-cup in it, trickling copiously on his head as it descended.

" Now, treasurer," cried Jack, " count up our cash and let us see how much we saved out of that pork-speculation."

Lucy went to *her* candle-box, at this suggestion, and bringing out a tin-case, laid the wealth of the Association before them. In scrip and pennies and half dimes they piled it up, counting over each other's shoulders.

" *Two* dollars ! " cried Jack with emphasis, "and twenty-five and twenty-five are fifty "—

" Three dollars," said Ben —

"And ten and ten and fifteen are thirty-five"—

"Just three dollars and seventy-five cents," decided Alice, rising from counting and beginning to clear away the dishes.

The Association looked around at itself rather sheepishly.

"Humph! you couldn't 'a bought that pig if you'd wanted to!" sneered Remus, the discomfitted furnisher of "points," with returning triumph.

"Three dollars wouldn't buy a six dollar pig!" added his twin, to strengthen his position.

"Well, we don't want a pig just yet, anyhow," laughed paternal Ben. "We'll wait awhile and get one some other way."

"I should like to inquire," said Jack, rising, as the treasurer with her Treasure and the secretary with her scrawled Constitution both disappeared to place their charges again in safety, "if this was a regular meeting? I was going to call a meeting of the Association to-night, and ask you all to my house!"

"*You* can't call a meeting: you aren't President."

"But I'm Vice. And the Vice-president has as much authority as the President in *our* Association!"

"Where is your house, Jack?" inquired Lucy, helping to whisk away the remains of the supper

"I want you all to come and see," cried Jack

"Arty knows. Don't you tell, Arty! I've got it all furnished and finished, and I'm going to begin housekeeping there right off."

Jack's eagerness having a strong effect upon the
Bunch, it was not long before the girls had their sup-
per-work done, and the house so tidy that any stray
neighbor who might peep in would have to admit that
the Dogberry children did not get on so badly! Then
they all ran out at Jack's heels, Arthur dragging only
a step behind him, Rome and Remus with arms interlaced, "hippity-hopping," Lucy undulating like a
young sapling tossed by a merry wind, and only Ben
and Alice pretending to saunter, and they sauntered
eagerly!

I said it was a two-sided village they lived in : it
was actually known as Old Town and New Town ;
the Old Town having been a pulseless collection of
twenty houses until a railroad, like a great artery
brought it new blood. Then every enterprising citi-
zen dragged his house to, or built a new one beside,
the railroad ; strangers came to live there also, thus
forming a modern village where all the business and
most of the living was done. But there were poor
people and old settled residents who preferred to
make no change, and still remained on the one old
street : this side of the village was therefore called

Old Town, and in spite of the three or four pretty
houses on it was a sad array of tumble-in roofs and
shaky dwellings.

The Dogberry Bunch lived in New Town, on the
eastern side of the railway. Jack led them over the
shady lawn which Nature had planted so plentifully
with trees, and the girls with mounds of verbenas
pansies and all the flowers which give one the dear
delight of digging loam in spring-time and wearing
bloom in summer-time. On one side of the lawn
was a croquet set which perhaps remains to this day
a monument of Dogberry ingenuity. The mallets
and balls Jack turned himself, and he and Ben set
up for wickets pieces of iron hoops off old tubs. As
a Bunch they were invincibly fond of croquet, and
being forbidden by their circumstances and Guardian
to spend money on the game, they had to achieve it
some other way, and Rome finally sewed little triumphant red-white-and-blue flags to stick on the tops
of the painted stakes. On this victorious field their
voices might be heard nearly every summer evening ;
but Jack now led them past it and down through the
gate upon the bank beside the railroad.

"We don't want to go to the station, Jack," cried
Alice hesitating, as the troop filed along.

"'Tisn't at the station," declared Jack.

"As like as anyway," observed Lucy with some suspicion, "he's playing a trick on us as he did on me one day. He told me if I'd run down here I'd see a Cardiff giantess on one of the gravel-flats, and he helped me on the car, and when I couldn't see anything but sand, he says, 'Why, here you are! Look at yourself! 'A Cardiff giantess!'" sniffed Lucy.

"'Deed I ain't playing any trick!" pleaded Jack, laughing. "Remus has seen my house. It's only a little further — right down there."

"Like the Air-Castle in our yard?" inquired Maude. "Have you any steps to go up into it?"

"Yes, it has steps, but it isn't a tree." And diving down the railroad bank, Jack cried: "Walk in ladies and gentlemen of the Dogberry 'Sociation! This is the House that Jack made!"

CHAPTER II.

THE HOUSE THAT JACK MADE, AND THE FIRST DOINGS IN IT.

JACK'S house was a caboose which had stood unused upon a side-track for some weeks. An old brick-red affair, with windows at the sides and a door at each end, boarded gaily and coolly, with blue inside. This thin coat of blue paint Jack had put on himself, from a paint pot in the station. The indulgent station-master, seeing the boy always active, let him amuse himself as he would in the intervals between business. And the result was that Jack applied himself to building a pleasure resort as other

men, oppressed by cares, apply themselves to creating
yachts, and country retreats and fancy gardens. The
sky-color extended over the floor also, and the walls
were relieved with heavily framed pictures of scenes
on different railway routes, exquisite prints of the
superior inducements one route offered above others,
and such other works of art as the young connois-
seur could get from the waiting-room in the depot.
That day he had also found time to make ropes of
leaves by fastening them together with pins of their
own stems, and these gala garlands hung in festoons
all around the car. Jack had a sofa, made on a sort
of locker, of two old cushions which used to belong
to his father's buggy. Several chairs borrowed from
the station stood along the walls, and the whole
place was in such up-and-down order as only bach-
elors admire. Jack helped his visitors up the rear
steps of his palace, and hustled them in with great
excitement.

"See, I can put these shutters to," he cried, "and
darken the room. There's a lamp in this box, and
there's the hook on the ceiling to swing it to! Allie,
I want you to make me some white curtains, like we
have at our windows. When it grows cold, maybe I
can put a stove up in here," soared Jack.

"Well, what a boy!" commented Allie's low contralto.

"This is quite a fine place," said Ben, "but if I'd go and set up in the Air-Castle now, and the girls and Rheem'd build shingle houses out among the trees, what would the house and the Bunch come to?"

Rome and Remus were in ecstacies with it, and begged Jack to let them play there every afternoon. Arthur gallopped up and down until the caboose shook, and then took up his station on a chair by one of the high windows to watch the depot, that haunt of locomotives which were the delight of his young soul.

"But what if a train should carry this off?" exclaimed Lucy.

"No danger," replied the master of the house that Jack made. "Mr. Joyce says it isn't needed. It won't be moved for a long while."

They all sat down and tried to fancy themselves going on a long journey in the caboose. "To California," suggested Jack, "and each of us owning a cam in a big gold mine."

"To some place in the mountains," said Lucy, "where the scenery would be lovely. And oh! I wish we could see the ocean!"

Ben expressed his preference for a city, while Alice desired a country continually flowering and maturing into fruit. Arthur, after listening to the others with wide-spread eyes, did not find his affections weaned from an imaginary place which he called "Hiddley-Giddle;" he was fond of telling strange tales every day about what he did in this place with two dream-play-mates to whom he **gave** the not very musical names of "Deedle" and "Sipsey." Deedle and Sipsey were anything he wanted them to be. They were boys or girls, or old men or dogs. If he disobeyed his elders it was because naughty Deedle or Sipsey "teased him to." They always lived in Hiddley-Giddle, and their unseen coming and going and his remarkable conversations with them amused the whole family who had out-grown the fancied play-mates which do seem to throng around an imaginative child of three years old.

"Let's have charades," said Rome and Remus, and the suggestion was no sooner made than the family divided, Ben with Alice and the baby withdrawing to sit on the railroad bank, the rest closing the shutters on that side the caboose and setting to work upon a "scene." One or two flying trips were made to the house for accoutrements, and then the audience was called up on the platform to see "a charade of two syllables and two scenes;" and the caboose door, thrown open disclosed

Scene First,

which was evidently a picture of William Tell. Rheem, with several cushions piled under him, made a brave little Gessler, and Loo beside him, with a broomstick held erect, a most formidable guard.

"Bring in the prisoner!" commanded Gessler, dimpling in spite of his ferocious character. The guard, Lucy, at once opened the box and produced Jack, who gritted his teeth, rolled his eyes, and in several other ways testified his dislike to the little tyrant.

"What's your name, Tell?" inquired Gessler.

"Tell yourself!" responded the prisoner.

"I told *you* to tell!"

"Well, then, Tell."

"Guard, give the prisoner a knock."

Guard knocked the prisoner, who howled like a school-boy, and pranced with great agility. This supple use of his person evidently reminded the tyrant of something which he immediately stated.

"I hear that you are very skillful in using the bow! I want to see you shoot an apple on your boy's head."

"I don't see his head," objected Tell.

"Guard, bring the boy and the apple."

Maude was brought from behind a chair, placed in position for supporting the apple, which was only the hollow gourd used for dipping water in the kitchen. This fruit being put upon her head, Tell without more ado produced a pea-shooter and peppered it heartily until the tyrant expressed himself satisfied, and the door closed.

" It's ' tell ' something," commented Ben. But presently the

SECOND SCENE

was uncurtained, and it seemed to be a version of "Lady Godiva."

Jack, with a bedquilt around him to represent lordly

MR. AND MRS. GODIVA.

robes, a tall black hat on his h e a d, the broom-stick in h i s hand, and a hatchet hanging from his belt, stalked about frowning, and after him came Lady Godiva in her sister A l i c e ' s longest dress and a shawl trailing from her shoulders.

After the pair promenaded the oppressed populace of Coventry, represented by Rheem in a pair of his big brother's which reached above his knees and holding a pillow-case and a towel to his eyes, and Maude weeping under a parasol.

" Mr. Godiva," pleaded my lady, "please don't tax these poor people so."

"I will tax them all I please!" cried Mr. Godiva, brandishing his broomstick.

" See how they cry!"

" Well, let them cry!   It's healthy!"

Here the oppressed populace howled.

"O, Mr. Godiva," cried my lady, "if you will promise not to tax the poor people so, I will get on a horse and ride clear through town!"

This proposition struck Mr. Godiva very favorably, and he grasped a chair to be used as my lady's steed. " Go ahead — I'll promise," said he.

Mr. Godiva then turned and spoke to the populace.

" Now, all of you hide your eyes and don't look at me, and you won't have to pay any taxes!"

The populace instantly retired to a corner and stuck their heads under a cushion, while Lady Godiva mounted her chair; and her lord divested himself of bedquilt and hatchet, and mounted another chair to stare her out of countenance in the character of Peeping Tom.   By the time the lady had galloped the length of the caboose, the populace, by peeping themselves, had become aware of his staring, and the descent they made on him again closed the door.

" Cry? Tax? What is it?" asked Alice of Ben
" Dear me! We mustn't let them be so noisy! All

the people in town will be coming to see what is the matter !"

Half a dozen boys, who were happy and ragged in their Saturday's release from school, and ready to interest themselves in whatever might turn up, were pressing up to the rear of the caboose; and resting their chins on the platform they saw the charade's final

TABLEAU.

A peculiar kind of sheep meandered out from some hiding-place in the caboose, with a buffalo robe tied around him and Jack's head appearing at one end; and after it came a smaller sheep in plaid shawl fleece and two paper horns over its bright eyes; and still another sheep, all white, with long blonde hair hanging over dark eye-lashes. It is impossible to tell all the pranks these sheep played. Their idea of a tableau was very animated ! They bleated and ran at each other; they skipped, and came down in a stiff-legged jump which was side-splitting. Over their pasture-fence of chairs they went with perfect disregard of their shins, the small sheep always following where the large one led. Great tableau, this !

At last, head down, and still frisking with the stiff-legged jump, they disappeared; and at once a distracted little shepherdess appeared, her short dress tucked up, her hat pushed back, and the broomstick again brought into play as her crook. The word was without doubt " Bo-Peep !" Wilhelm Tell's " bow " (which seemed unfair as he used a pea-shooter) and Tom's " peep " made the charade.

The town ragamuffins applauded so heartily, and were so eager to introduce themselves into the caboose, that they soon excluded Jack's first guests. It was growing dusk, and a breathless heat stifled the landscape.

" We shall have a storm to-night, I believe," said one of the Bunch, as they all, excepting Jack, strolled back to the house.

He came later, while they sat in the Air-Castle and on the stoop, to tell them he meant to sleep in his own house that night :

" You better come home, dear," said Alice, who, high in the old tree where a seat was fixed, called by the children their " Air-Castle," could see heat-lightnings play and a dark hood of cloud drawing up from the west. " It's going to storm to-night."

Well, if it stormed cats and dogs, Jack would be as snug in the caboose as in his bed at home !

So he went back and secured his windows on the west, leaving only one on the east and a ventilator ajar for air ; and the rest of the Bunch went in and shut up their house.   In the midnight some of them were awakened by blinding light and by the groans of trees, and spouts of rain beating as if to wash their little dwelling into some universal ocean.

CHAPTER III.

"O, WHERE, O, WHERE —"

WHEN Benjamin arose in the morning and made the fire in the little back summer kitchen to heat the kettle for breakfast, he looked out on one of the most beautiful and burnished Sunday mornings this world has ever seen. The air was clear enough to make fairy spectacles of ; the very grass blades were strings of brilliants of the first water ; the roads were beaten out as firm and clean as granite.

One by one the Dogberrys appeared, each looking

as live and burnished as if just out of a storm-bath, also. Excepting Jack, who did not come. The table was laid, and they all sat down on their chairs in a great circle, and sang one of Philip Phillips' songs about the "Home of the Soul," their souls fairly dancing on the music because they were such a comfortable Bunch. Then all their knees plumped down on the floor at once, and they said the Lord's Prayer as one man, Rome and Remus kneeling opposite each other at the same chair, and almost knocking noses with fervor, their eyes being shut. They rose up and the Treasurer of the 'Sociation, according to Sunday morning custom, brought pennies from the fund and laid them on the table ready for Arthur, or whoever took his turn that day, to carry to Sunday-school.

Still Jack did not come.

"I b'lieve he's going to sleep all day," cried Rheem.

"Maybe something's happened!" cried Rome, spreading her black eye-lashes.

"Run and call him," said Alice.

"And tell him to hurry," added Loo, the house-keeper. "We sha'n't have much time to get the work done before Sunday-school."

You may picture to your mind's eye this Bunch

starting to Sunday-school in the respectable ways they had been trained to: all in pairs, or threes, or a group, all jolly, and somewhat proper in their good clothes, the mothers of the village looking after them with pride, and the fathers nodding smilingly.

"I wonder if our young ones would get along as well," says Mother Thomas, a large, generous woman, to her husband, a wizened, gray, ailing man, "if we had to leave 'em?"

"I don't know," he groans, "if they had my health all the time, they couldn't do much."

"Good-morning, little Bunch," says Mother Darling, the doctor's wife, a smiling, black-eyed woman, rustling past them with her last baby all dressed in white. "I have a nice big mess of peas for your dinner if some of you will come over and get it directly after Sunday-school."

"Them young ones does beat all!" says big John White, whittling a fence-rail and talking stock with a brother stock-shipper, but never failing to laugh a sort of benediction on the Bunch as they go by.

In this way the neighbors in the village take kindly notice of them. But to-day different ejaculations will be heard, for the Dogberry Bunch is broken and a Berry has dropped out.

Rome and Remus came running from their errand

of calling Jack, like two young hens. Now Rheem
fell down and Rome tumbled over him, and as soon
as she gained her feet, her twin made a dash and
tumbled over her.   But neither of them heeded these
mishaps.   Sprawled on the floor, they both gasped
out to the astonished family :

" *Jack's gone !* "

"Gone where ? " in chorus.

"Don't know ! He ain't there ! "

" Did you look in the caboose ? "

" THE CABOOSE IS GONE ! "

All Dogberry-dom now stood up, and let the breakfast alone, excepting Arthur who was in his high-
chair, and who required a good reason for leaving it.

"Why, where *is* the caboose ? " asked bewildered
Ben.

"Maybe the lightnin' struck it ! "   " Maybe it's
burnt up ! " from the twins.

" It's been taken off somewhere by trains in the
night ! " exclaimed convinced Lucy.   " I just told
him so ! "

"Where's Jack ? " cried Alice.

That was the question — where was Jack ?

" Just as like as not they've poured a whole lot of
grain — or hogs — in on him and smothered him ! "
said Rome beginning to brim with tears.

"Especially the hogs," observed Ben, "which would certainly smother if poured very fast!"

"I don't think it's funny a bit!" cried Rome.

"I don't either. But they don't load cabooses.

JACK'S GONE!

And I don't see how Jack could sleep while the cars were jarring. Pshaw! maybe it isn't gone at all! It blew like anything last night. The caboose may have rolled farther down the track."

They all ran to see. Up and down the rails with

their hands shielding their eyes from the morning sun, they looked and scampered. Some disabled old coal-flats and one box car lay on the switch. These, and nothing more.

Ben ran to Mr. Joyce, the station-master, and the rest of the Bunch, not knowing what else to do, ran after him. Mr. Joyce had been kept up late, and their loud raps at his door lasted some time before he appeared. He was a pleasant-faced man and laughed when he saw how he was besieged.

"Why, what's the matter?"

"Where's Jack, Mr. Joyce?"

"Home, isn't he?"

"No, sir. He slept in that caboose he fixed up for his house, last night —"

"And it's gone!" howled Maude.

Arthur by this time began to understand the calamity which had befallen his house, and having missed his favorite all the morning, now puckered up his face and set up a yell which brought the whole street to the doors.

Mr. Joyce seized his station key and hurried to the little freight-house and depot. He searched everywhere and looked puzzled. He looked up and down the track, but the red caboose was gone.

"Well, upon my word!" he exclaimed, while a

more doleful note came from the depressed Bunch.

" Hush, Arty ! " soothed Alice, " Jacky isn't hurt."

" Why, no," cried Joyce, " but I don't see how it happened ! There was a fearful storm when that last freight was making up. They had a lot of empty box cars to take up here. The caboose must have got run in among them. It was a through freight for Cincinnati. I'll inquire along the road."

He went to the instrument, and while it clicked the disconsolate Dogberry Bunch hearkened and thought of their absent Berry.

" You better go home, and don't be frightened," said Mr. Joyce. " It'll be sometime before I get an answer. I'll let you know where he is as soon as I find out, and I'll have them search Number 5. If it made a good run, it'll be in Cincinnati this afternoon. Don't you be scared, Jack can take care of himself. I'll send a message to the depot-master of the C. H. & D. road, and he'll look after Jack when he gets there."

" Thank you, Mr. Joyce," said Sweet Alice solemnly, turning the head of the party homeward, and leading Arthur by the hand.

" Where's Jack ? " cried the poor little fellow continually. " I want him. I want my Jack ! "

And everybody failing to produce his favorite, he

sat down on the road and beat the rails with all the might of his little heels, the angry blood flushing even his head till it glowed like a turkey's through his hair.

"Get up, Arty," begged Loo, tremulously. "Brother will come back pretty soon."

"I want him now!" howled the baby.

"Let's go and hunt Jacky," volunteered Maude.

"Where?" yielded the youngster, allowing himself to be stood up, and his petticoats to be brushed. "Will we go on train? where's big engine? where we hunt Jack, Romey?"

"O, pshaw! Jack's all right," said Ben easily, as they trooped under the trees and re-entered their dwelling.

And beginning to see the whole affair in the light of a joke, the family at this point broke out laughing, and sat down gaily to breakfast; still, with the exception of the little brother in skirts, who asked at intervals, "*Where* Jacky gone? *where* him gone?"

"Gone off with Deedle and Sipsey," replied Rheem, bantering the baby, "gone to Hiddley-Giddle."

"What's this?" cried Mother Darling, the doctor's wife, running in with the baby half-dressed, its dimples huddled in a shawl; "they say Jack got carried off by a freight train last night. Is it so?"

"Yes'm," replied the Bunch, laughing; and Ben rose to place a chair for the little mother.

" What's happened to you young ones?" exclaimed

ARTY.

brawny Mother Thomas, sailing in with her portly air.

The story was told over again, and the mothers also

reassured them as Mr. Joyce had done. They held quite a levee, their neighbors ran in and out so, until the small bell of the small white church rang for Sabbath-school. Mr. Joyce sent a message that he could find out nothing certain about Jack, but everything was certainly going well with Number 5, or he would hear it over the wires.

The Bunch was broken for the day. They went straggling.

"Where's Arthur?" inquired Alice, shaking out her parasol as she and Loo started.

"Gone with Rome and Rheem, I think."

Rome and Rheem were walking primly along talking of the great event which had disturbed the nineteenth century that day. Maude's finery consisted principally of a lilac silk mantilla which had belonged to her mother. Her eyes expanded like two headlights over her Sunday gear, when the question of Arthur's whereabouts was put.

"Why, didn't Mrs. Darling take him when she came along with the baby? Oh, maybe *he's* lost too!"

The idea! But he was not in the little whitewashed church, where the village children were singing joyfully through their noses. Mother Darling, when whispered to, did not know anything about him. Ben, being summoned from the "Youth's

Bible Class," ran to every house in search of him.

Then the town was roused.

It was funny for a live, big boy like Jack to be carried off in the night : people could grin at such a mishap ; but when the three-year-old of the town's prize orphans disappeared as suddenly as if dropped in a pit, the Bunch's bereavement looked startling. Several fathers went to work dragging their cisterns : a group went to examine Sugar Creek.

There was at one end of the street which formed Old Town a tottering shell which once served as a tavern ; but being forsaken by every respectable creature in the place, was now the haunt of all sorts of wretches. More than a dozen families crowded it. It was fit to compare with city tenements ; and this swarming den was known as the "Beehive." Tramps passing through the town, made this their stopping-place. A stoop composed of rotting boards was in front of it, and a different colored rag appeared at every window, from which nearly all sash and glass were broken.

John White hurried to the "Beehive" to ask them about little Arthur. The Bees, although their neighbors took so little interest in them, felt a lazy interest in their neighbors, and were generally peeping out of the Beehive or buzzing on the stoop, to see what

might be going on in the town. To-day being Sunday and no trains running, they were out in strong
force, smoking, and blinking their cadaverous eyes —
gaunt, nerveless-looking men, dirty and only half
alive. Women's voices, scolding, made the inside of
the " Beehive " ring. Some playful young Bees
played marbles and pulled hair at one end of the
stoop.

" How d'ye do," said easy John White to the men
who pulled out their pipes and listened with calm pat-
ronage to their wealthier neighbor. " Have you seen
anything of a little fellow around here ? The Dogberry children have lost their baby — about three
years old — chap in petticoats."

" When — did — they — lose — him ? " inquired
one of the Bees with a slow drawl : they were above
excitement.

" Missed him a couple of hours or so ago, but
don't remember seeing him since breakfast. One of
them dressed him for Sunday-school before breakfast ; and then one of the boys got run off on a
freight, and it excited them so they forgot about the
little fellow."

The Bees pulled their pipes silently, as if they had
all found first-rate honey-tubes.

" He had on a little linen dress," continued John ;

' thinnish child ; blue eyes, light : I expect you know him. I'm afraid he's found the creek! You haven't seen anything of him ? "

"Saw — a — little — young one," volunteered one deliberate drone, "go — past — with — a —woman — 's morning. Didn't —stop — here."

"*I* — saw — him," added another Bee. "Thought — she — was — playin'— with him. Movers —over — in — the — woods — last — night."

"Light child — linen dress ? " asked John White.

"Ye — es," drawled the Bee.

"The Dogberry baby, do you think ? "

I — thought — it— was — him."

John White made haste to carry this news, and several men got upon horses and galloped in the direction the movers' caravan was said to have taken. As he supposed, the strollers were only agueish Indianians trailing away to some point farther west. Their wagon was covered with canvass stretched on hoops, and drawn by horses paired like David and Goliah, fearfully thin, and Goliah wheezing as if every breath must be his last. Inside the wagon cowered the usual hollow-cheeked settler, his care-worn wife and fifteen children, in various stages of chills-and-fever. It was too great a satire to suppose such a man had picked up the missing boy, but the men inquired if he had seen a stray child. The settler had not seen any stray child. His wife, kind soul, was full of sympathy when she heard a child was lost, and counted her fifteen over with a more thankful heart.

They hunted New Town and Old Town, they dragged the creek above and below the dam, they searched the woods: the long summer afternoon wore away and night came, and still little Arthur Dogberry was not found.

CHAPTER IV

THE RAILROAD MUTINY.

WHEN Jack awoke in the caboose, he was astonished by a roaring and rumbling and also by the motion which shook him to and fro. He had heard the storm in the night, but this was not the sound of a storm. His bristling hair fairly stood on end as he recognized the grinding whirr of wheels. Opening a shutter, he poked his head into the dark and dodged back just in time to avoid the scaffolding of a bridge they were passing.

"Yes, sir!" said Jack, sitting down to his convictions, "this caboose has started on its travels, and has
invited Mr. J. Dogberry to go along. Thank you,
ma'am. My health was needing a little trip. I *bet*
they'll laugh at home! Loo'll never forget it! She'll
keep it to pay me back for the Cardiff giantess with!
She said I'd get run off. I wonder what Arty'll do?
Which way is this train going?"

He opened the door at one end, and saw a blank
wall of freight running in front of him; he opened
the door at the other end and made out a similar
sight. The landscape was lightening: he could make
out trees and high gravelled banks.

Jack shut the door, and sitting down by an open
shutter, enjoyed his trip. The explanation which Mr.
Joyce had given the children occurred to him: his
caboose was taken up among empty freight cars:
these would be thrown off on some switch or other
track, and he must watch his chances for a return
journey. He heartily enjoyed his adventure.

Toward morning the rattling train ran into a sad,
bedraggled town. The storm was left far behind,
and it is probable that Jack the Nimble would have
climbed to the tops of the freights long before and
made acquaintance with every man having them in
charge, if the novelty of his position had not kept
him still.

There seemed to be a lock in the progress of the train. Jack saw the the name " Pontiac " in large black letters over the depot door. Several other trains were massed on switches and tracks leading to different points of the compass. Pontiac, dark

JACK.

and draggled as it appeared, was something of a railroad centre. The train stood still, but nothing was loading, nothing cast off.

It was now nearly Sunday morning. " Perhaps this is the end of the trip," said Jack, " but I thought our

Number 5 was a through freight for Cincinnati."

He stepped down into the coal dust and wandered along the train.   It was now that very dark hour just before day-dawn : a knot of men with a lantern were muttering near the engine.   One, grimed but commanding, was certainly the engineer;   the others brakemen of this and other trains massed at Pontiac. They were complaining bitterly of measures taken by the Company who owned the road.   As Jack heard them he felt they were half in the right : their money was overdue ; they were threatened with a reduction of pay, and they would strike!   So far so good. Young Dogberry silently endorsed all he heard.   He thought right was right, whether on his side or on the side of the man who employed him.   If a man would not pay for service he ought to suffer inconvenience and loss by having the service taken from him without warning.   But pretty soon some more men came up, of the very worst sort.   Whether they were railroad employés or vagrants, Jack could not make out.   They talked as if they owned the roads and were masters of the roads' interests, but Jack considered himself a railroad employé, and he would not have classed himself with these men.   They had a lot of oil and matches, and mentioned "firing" and "breaking," and excited the others, excepting one who went and sat down on the side of a platform.

Jack followed him.

"What they going to do?" he asked.

The brakeman replied rather indifferently that he didn't know: raise the old Satan likely.

"But this freight that came down from Chicago — oughtn't it to go on?"

The brakeman laughed, and said it ought to throw off half the empty boxes and take on four or five cars of cattle to run into Cincinnati: "but the engineer is drunk," he added, "and they're all on a strike, him at the head of them. I don't know how it'll end. I don't intend to have nothing to do with it if I can help it, but if I'm forced in I'll have to do as the others do. All that I'm afraid of is that they are going to make mischief, and destroy property. The Road *hasn't* treated us fair. Still, burning stock is dirty business."

"No, I don't like that, myself," said Jack maturely, "and I think this train ought to be got through. It's pretty near Sunday morning. We've been here over an hour."

"What train do you belong to?" inquired the brakeman.

Jack explained his presence, and then added "as all the rest are deserting, don't you think we could get it through ourselves?"

The train-hand laughed.

"Well," exclaimed the boy, "I know all about an engine. The engineers on our road have taken me up and down. I ain't in the railroad business for nothing, I tell ye! Don't you suppose I've picked up everything?"

At this moment a yell was raised by some of the men in mutiny.

"I wish I was home in the city," said the brakeman discontentedly.

"You just wait a bit!" cried Jack, dashing into the telegraph office. Here a sleepy young man, disturbed and inefficient, had just finished sending over the wires to headquarters an account of the disturbances pending.

Jack seized a telegraph blank and hastened to write:

"Engineer and all but one man of through freight Number 5, have struck: going to be a fuss. I can bring it through all right, with orders.

J. DOGBERRY."

"Who sends this message?" inquired the operator, eyeing the young man.

"Dogberry, sir."

In the midst of the impending riot which Pontiac's

small muster of police could never quell, the operator did not inquire minutely about Dogberry, but secretly commending him for keeping out of sight, sent his message. Before the last click, a frowsy man rushed in.

" It's all up," he exclaimed, " we can't get out of here unless the Company sends me another engineer, and there'll be worse mischief yet before one can come ! Got my orders ? "

" Have 'em in a few minutes," replied the operator. " Man here offered to take your train through."

From this conversation Jack understood that the man was the conductor of Number 5, and he waited as breathlessly as the conductor for orders. In a few minutes the answer came. The conductor was ordered to put Engineer Dogberry in the cab and to proceed at once. Dogberry's orders were minute. The conductor seized them.

" There's his fireman over there," said the operator pointing to Jack.

The conductor thrust the orders into his hand.

" There's one brakeman I can rely on," he exclaimed, " he and I will attend to the coupling. In ten minutes we want to pick up these cattle cars and be out of here ! "

He ran in one direction, Jack in the other. The

boy leaped into the cab, piled fuel in his furnace, and made a quick examination of his locomotive. The orders were very brief and plain; he had them by heart in a moment.

A few faint streaks began to appear in the east, and a general light diffused itself. Jack ran his engine and the cars attached, forward, and at a signal backed upon a switch and took up the waiting stock. These movements were so sudden and unexpected, that he was really under way before the groups of rough men saw that a train was moving out. Some of them were talking of heaping the freights and setting them on fire. The engineer who forsook Number 5, came leaping along beside the train, flushed with anger and drink. He caught sight of the little fellow in his engine cab and yelled at him. He looked so furious and all the running men looked so furious that J. Dogberry was roused through every molecule of his blood. These men might try to throw things under the wheels and so ditch the train: a shot was fired, the ball splintering a panel of the cab; I only do Jack justice when I say he hardly thought of the ball — his mind was taken up with the results of a disaster if disaster there should be. He put on a full head of steam, and the empty freights and cattle cars sailed away! He was now accountable for the train — he a mere boy ! — when the Company probably thought they were entrusting it to a man and a licensed locomotive engineer. The thing he had undertaken with the best but unconsidered impulses, now looked very startling. Still, Jack knew what he was about, and his iron horse in a twinkling was out of Pontiac and sailing along over the open country. The Road was certainly a mismanaged one, but at that time discontent among the employés was not general. There were no other strikes on the line, and safe out of Pontiac, the men having the train in charge anticipated no other trouble than stoppages caused by their delay.

Morning advanced. Jack stood up to his business, his determined eye watching the road ahead, his hand testing the steam gauge, or with the whistle warning distant stray animals off the track. Through forest and across highways, as the day grew brighter around him, over river bridges, and along green corn-fields, he roared on and on !

Everything going smoothly, the conductor left the rear, ran along the tops of the cars, leaping gaps between them, dropped into the tender and entered the engine-cab.

He looked all around, holding back the congratulatory speech ready on his lips.

"Hullo, fireman, where's Dogberry?"

"Here, sir."

"The engineer, I mean.   Man that run us out of Pontiac?"

"*I'm the man,*" says Jack, examining the steam gauge again.   Upon which the conductor sat down.

"You little rat!" said he at last.   "If you hadn't been so plucky I'd pitch you and your cheek off the train!"

CHAPTER V.

"ONE BY ONE BEYOND RECALL."—*Song.*

"LAW me! what *has* become of the child!" whispered Mother Dr. Darling in an awe-struck voice, as she tossed her own white clean baby among the panic-filled Dogberrys who were left. She and Mrs. Thomas and a few other neighbors were talking apart. Ben and Sweet Alice sat by the table; she with her head down, he looking dazed and pale. Loo stood by the window

53

shaking with sobs, while Rome and Remus were making the air melodious in a similar manner, in the kitchen.

It was Monday evening, and the townspeople had given Arty up. They agreed that he had been carried away. The old Bee of the " Beehive," who claimed to have seen the child with a woman, when closely questioned was not sure of anything. It was all a paralyzing mystery. Joyce kindly telegraphed both ends of the road inquiring for a stray child. They could not find him in Sugar Creek or the mill pond. At thought of the little fellow down in the slime or gravel, his rigid hands clinched on dead leaves, the elder Dogberrys were frantic. It was also maddening to think he might be in the hands of some evil-minded person who abused him—he might be hungry or sick.

" Is Ben, or is Miss Alice in ? " asked Mr. Joyce, stepping upon the door-stone.

Ben and Alice were both at the door, and under their elbows pressed the twins, while Mothers Thomas and Darling pressed at their backs.

" Have you heard anything ? " inquired Alice, wiping her eyes. It was poor little Arty's funeral without his body left as a visible sign of consolation.

" I've got a telegram from Danport," said Joyce.

"There was a child picked up there to-day — hurt on the streets."

Rome and Remus uttered a mournful howl; they had no doubt the hurt child was Arthur.

"Name not known," continued Joyce; "the child was run over and unconscious. Taken to the house of a lady named Greenoff."

"Aunt Greenoff!" exclaimed the five Dogberrys in awe.

Alice turned to Ben.

"We'd better go and see if it's Arty," said Ben.

"Of course!" cried Mother Darling eagerly, "take our buggy: the Doctor is riding horse-back now."

"And put our sorrel into it," added Mother Thomas; "he's a good traveler. Thomas isn't using him for anything."

Now Danport was an old rich town, lying only twelve miles distant; its railroad connection with the new village, however, was roundabout and included several delays and changes of cars. People seldom thought of going to Danport, therefore, otherwise than by their own conveyances.

"Yes, and just you get ready right away," added one of the neighbors, "and we'll get some supper for you."

The neighborly hands made themselves busy, some preparing the meal, others putting Alice into her best

dress, her black alpaca and making up a bundle of
such things as the young Heads of the house might
need.   It was now her vacation, so she could leave
the school.   Presently Ben drove up the Doctor's
buggy and Thomas' stiff, old sorrel.   Then he hurried
into his Sunday suit, and the shattered family sat
down to a quick meal, Mother Darling and Mother
Thomas waiting on them as if they were so many
babies, and these good women were particularly fond
of babies.

"We'll be back as quick as we can," said Alice to
the three Berries left.   "Rheemie and Maud, you
mind Loo, and all take care of yourselves."

Just as Ben gathered the lines off old sorrel's back,
and began to drive off, John White came running,
waving his hand to stop them.   He drew out a very
large pocket-book before reaching the buggy.

"Going to Danport to see if Arty's there, eh? Ben,
you'll need some money.   How much have you?"

Ben colored.   He didn't know, but guessed he had
about a dollar and a half in his purse.

"Pshaw! that won't pay a livery bill, to say nothing of other expenses you may have.   I want to loan
you ten dollars.   Take both bills: if you don't need
'em you can bring 'em back, you know.   That's all.
I won't stop you any longer."

"How good everybody is!" said Allie, leaning back

on the stuffed cushions of Dr. Darling's old carriage, as if it was the full heart of humanity beating under her; "we hadn't time to draw my money, and I didn't even think of it."

The mothers of the town withdrew to their own homes, and Lucy and the twins sat down on the front stoop, forlorn and watching.

"I wonder if 'twas Arty?" questioned Rheem.

"He's hurt awful bad!" snuffed Maude.

"I don't believe *'twas* Arty. Aunt Greenoff," said the boy, handling his strange relative's name with great respect, "would send us word."

"*She* wouldn't know Arty," said Loo sadly. "She never saw him in her life. She doesn't know much about any of us."

"What makes her our aunt?" propounded Rome.

"She isn't. She's a cousin, or something, of mother's. We've always been poor and her folks were always rich. That's why she never came to see us," explained Lucy simply, and without the least bitterness.

Next morning while the three children sat at breakfast, Mr. Joyce stepped up on the stoop with more telegraphic news.

He looked puzzled.

"There's a child exactly answering Arty's descrip

tion," said he, " up in Carver City. A tramping
woman brought him in."

" What'll we do ? " cried Loo. " Ben and Alice are
gone to Danport."

" Let *me* go to Carver City," said Remus.

" And me," added Rome.

" Lucy had better go," suggested Mr. Joyce, " and
you two little fellows keep house. There's the half-
past eight passenger coming. I can put you on that
and you'll get back on the four o'clock accommoda-
tion. They stop here half an hour for breakfast."

In half an hour, therefore, Lucy, the house-mother,
forsook her charge and set out in search of that
other charge. The Dogberrys had been steadily
decreasing like John Brown's little Indians, and now
the twins sat by themselves, too anxious to play
heartily, in a sort of Sabbath day of expectancy.
Rome got some dinner of bread and butter, berries
and cold beef, which Remus solemnly helped her
despatch. And shortly after a very little fellow from
the " Beehive " peeped around the door-post.

" Say ! " saluted the urchin.

" Hullo, Jacey ! Come in," said the host.

" No, I don't want to. Come out here."

What is that free-masonry among boys which refuses
roofing ? Your brother's chum comes and whistles

for him, and, obedient as a dog, he springs from his place and runs out to answer the whistle. If Julia or Dora should stand on the pavement and whistle for *you*, how you would resent the girl's breeding and impertinence! " Does she think I'm going to run to her? Indeed! let her ring the bell, or come in at the side door!" Brother Tom, however, will gallop half a square to encounter his signal-giver. And although Rheem was not intimate with Jacey Dixon from the

JACEY DIXON AND THE TWINS.

" Beehive," that request to see him out of doors struck home at once, aud he went out to consult Jacey.

"You found yer little brother?" asked Jacey, by way of introducing the subject, and wiping his nose the whole length of his arm as he spoke.

"No. Ben and Alice have gone to Danport and Loo's gone to Carver City—"

" Well, he ain't neither place. I bet I know just where he is!"

"I bet you don't!" cried Remus, becoming excited.

Maude came to the door and joined in the consultation. And the result was that the little house was left alone, without one Dogberry in it, standing silent and lonesome in the pleasant summer afternoon. A barren stem — the Berries all rolling away.

CHAPTER VI.

HEN Mr. Joyce put Loo upon the train for Carver City he had in his hand a message from Jack, but the new interest concerning Arthur put it out of his mind so he forgot even to mention it to her. The message said:

"MR. JOYCE: I got carried off in the caboose. Am in Cincinnati. Tell our children am coming back just as soon as possible.

"JACK DOGBERRY."

61

Loo had in her pocket the money she made selling strawberries and which she had been saving for a new dress. But when the train started and the conductor came to her and spoke about her little lost brother, and she produced her worn portmonnaie, he said it "was all right." Joyce was sending her up on his pass; and he, the conductor, would speak to the conductor of the return train about her. Loo thanked him and sat still, feeling awed by the unaccustomed rush at which she was going, and fixing in her mind the course Mr. Joyce told her to take when she reached Carver City. She was to inquire of the station-master the way to the Dubbs House, and at the Dubbs House for a little boy about three years old, taken by the authorities from a tramping woman to be held until called for by his friends.

The smoky houses, dirty suburbs and pert city affectation of the town of Carver soon appeared. Bewildered Lucy was helped off the train politely by the conductor and followed the other passengers into the depot. After some inquiry she found the person who had charge of the depot, and he sent an employé to show her to the Dubbs House. Entering that lordly brick pile, amid the sounding of dinner-gongs and the rush of cheerful people more at home away from home than she, Loo stood anxiously in a vestibule while the messenger inquired at the clerk's office. Presently a waiter led her up-stairs to a parlor.

"When was that little child left here?" was the inquiry passed from the clerk's office to the proprietor, and from the proprietor to his various assistants.

Into the very parlor where Loo sat huddled up on a stiff sofa, a little boy came bouncing, and immediately after him a woman with her hat and gloves in her hand. She seemed unable to let the child get out of her sight and called him shrilly when he peeped out upon the balcony. As she was drawing on her gloves a very pleasant gentleman appeared and walked up to Loo.

"Yes," said he, "here you are. This is the little boy, and he has just been claimed by his friends who are taking him away."

Loo looked hard at the child. There was no sign of Arty about him. He had bluff blue eyes and dark hair, and was fat and boisterous. She wondered if she wasn't forgetting how Arty looked — he had been lost so long! She took out her handkerchief and wiped her eyes and then noticed that the child's mamma was regarding her keenly, as if suspicious that *she* might be another vagrant after that precious little son.

"This young Miss's brother has been lost or

stolen, also," explained the kind proprietor of the Dubbs House. "Lost since yesterday morning, eh?"

"Sunday morning," sobbed Loo.

"I am very sorry we haven't him here, too," said the proprietor, and then a waiter called him out.

As soon as the recovered child's mamma understood the state of the case she went and sat by Loo, asking a thousand questions, even shedding tears with her own calamity so fresh in mind. She went away reluctantly and had her boy kiss Loo so many times at parting, that the youngster lost patience and roared indignantly until he was out of hearing.

Hours must pass before Lucy could return home. She did not think of dinner, but walked out of the Dubbs House and wandered about the streets, wondering if Ben and Alice also had found somebody else's child.

Ben and Alice hastened along in Dr. Darling's buggy, drawn by Thomas' good old sorrel, which put the miles behind him as fast as any sorrel need to. The lamplighter was just touching up the street gas in Danport as they drove in, looking each out at a side of the conveyance and timid about what they ought to do.

"Do you know where Mrs. Greenoff lives?" in

quired Ben of the lamplighter, as that cantering gentleman mounted a lamp on the curb at which he drew
up sorrel.

" Right there," answered the man, indicating a residence whose face he had just illuminated, and so
saying he cantered on.

It was a brown-stone front with a flight of broad steps
guarded by lions in stone.   Lace drapery shaded the
lights within.   If Ben and Alice had not been so
anxious about Arthur, their simple country feet must
have felt shy on the steps of this palace.   Ben tied
sorrel to a ring in the pavement and mounted to the
door with his sister.

A very neat girl opened the door to them, and
showed a vast expanse of hall melting away into a
flight of velvet-covered stairs.

" Is Mrs. Greenoff at home?" trembled Ben's
voice.

" I believe she is," replied the servant doubtfully.

" We have come to see if a little child we heard
was hurt here, was our little brother."

Inspecting them quickly and with surprise, the
girl showed them into a small room on the left side
of the hall, which was evidently Mrs. Greenoff's morning-room and library.   Black walnut shelves filled
two opposite sides of the room, where books stood

shoulder against shoulder in rich array. The top of the shelves glistened with china ; there were rare old cups, so thin that their closely wrought pictures seemed painted on air ; green and brown majolica in pug dogs and tall, glistening vases ; fanciful faïence, and pitchers of purest porcelain ; and on a round table was a brown-red chocolate tête-á-tête set, which looked as if it had been used within the hour : in fact, it was Mrs. Greenoff's habit to order chocolate into the library every evening before dinner-time. There were easy-chairs of every description. The padded floor drowned every step. And, stooping from the centre of the high, frescoed ceiling, a bronze Hymen held out two torches of gas ; one a mere star, the other a clear flame, which revealed fully the names of the books in the cases, the pictures, and a marble copy of the Medicean Venus.

"Do you think Arty is *here?*" whispered poor Sweet Alice.

" I — don't — know," was all Ben Bolt could reply.

They waited some minutes. Ben squatted on a camp-stool, balancing himself carefully, Alice sinking deeper and deeper into a velvet chair.

"Isn't it lovely here ?" said Alice again. "She must be so rich, Ben ! "

The door opened and "she" entered: Mrs. Greenoff,

widow. A slight, very stylish, very handsome lady, with eyes which were black and keen when she wished to be penetrating, and brown and soft when she wished to be winning. Her silk garments clung close and statuesque around her, without trailing and without much rustle. Her white, fine hands glittered with the liquid white of diamonds. Her eyes were black and penetrating as she looked at the children when they rose up before her. Ben's camp-seat rose part of the way with him and tumbled back in a collapse. His face turned red, but he stood up finely and holding his hat in his hand, made his bow.

"We are the Dogberry children," said Ben.

"Indeed," said Mrs. Greenoff.

"Yes, ma'am. And Arty, our youngest, got lost Sunday morning; and Mr. Joyce, that's the agent in New Town, got a telegram that there was a little boy here. So we came to see if it was he."

Ben used his best grammar and held himself as became the Head of the Bunch. Inwardly he was slightly nettled at the lady's manner, and though he admired her intensely he wished her to see he came on business and for nothing else.

But Mrs. Greenoff now came forward and took both children by the hand.

"I have not seen you since you were babies," said

she, "but I am glad to see Sarah Dogberry's children. I have often thought of looking after you,
but matters of one kind or another always prevented
me. Yes, there was a little child hurt on this street
this morning and I have him up-stairs. I do not
know your little brother, but I am afraid — I do not
know whether to say I am afraid, or I hope, it is he.
Come up with me quietly and you may see him. But
don't agitate him. He is asleep now. An omnibus
ran over him," continued Mrs. Greenoff, leading them
up the padded stairs and along another vast, dimly
lighted hall, "but, fortunately, he was only knocked
down and bruised a little. Still, he is such an ex-
citable child the doctor says he must be kept quiet
as possible, or the strong emotions he has been under
will produce fever."

She opened a door into a cool, high room which
suggested glaciers and mountains and cascades to a
travelled mind, but to Ben and Alice it suggested
nothing but Arty. A quiet woman with a broad lap,
in a black dress and white apron, rose, obeying a
sign from Mrs. Greenoff, and drew the curtain
back off a large crib standing in the middle of
the room. There he lay. It was Arty! His delicate
face was flushed and every hair on his head glinted
in the old way. Bless the wax-like hands folded on

the counterpane! Bless his dear mouth! Bless his downy, golden eyebrows and the lashes flaring so

IT WAS ARTY!

from his lids! Alice could scarcely keep from flying at him and squeezing him to her heart's content. Now that he *was* alive and safe and not badly hurt, his young foster-parents realized what a huge weight of suspense they had carried. Ben groaned joyfully. The nurse, understanding the case, smiled sympathizingly; and two crystal tears rolled from Alice's eyes down her clear cheeks.

"She is quite a pretty little thing," thought Mrs. Greenoff. She motioned them to follow her out again and they reluctantly descended the stairs after her.

"He is really doing very well," said she. "I am exceedingly glad he was brought to this house."

"When can we take him back?" asked Ben.

Mrs. Greenoff laughed.

"My dear boy, I don't intend to let that baby go away under a week. Indeed, the doctor says he must not be farther moved and excited. Now, let me make you comfortable. How did you come?"

"In Dr. Darling's buggy. It's hitched out in front."

Mrs. Greenoff went across the library and pulled a silk tassel which hung from the ceiling.

"Well then, ma'am," pursued Ben, "we thank you very much indeed; and if you and the doctor think he had better be let stay, Allie and I would better go right back and tell the other children, and we can keep coming to see him till he comes home."

A respectful man entered and stood for orders; to whom Mrs. Greenoff turned and said:

"Michael, there is a buggy at the door which you will attend to."

Michael having passed out, the lady further continued:

"My dears, don't shame me because I have been so tardy about showing interest in you. You will remain with me to-night — and perhaps to-morrow —

at anyrate. You can write a message at once and I will have it sent to the family. Go in there if you want to wash your hands. Dinner will be ready shortly." She pulled a curtain one side and showed them a cunning room with marble basins and plenty of towels, where water followed the turn of a faucet. This bath-room communicated with Mrs. Greenoff's own apartment, and was the connecting and rejuvenating link which united her morning hours to her morning-room.

" My patience, Ben ! " murmured Alice as she rinsed her fingers and watched the water curl away, " how does she stand it till this time without dinner ? "

"I guess it's the same as tea," replied Ben, "only she calls it dinner."

It was not the same as tea, however, as they found when they were ushered into the dining-room. It was an exquisite meal in courses, containing dishes of which the children had never heard. There were five plates laid. Mrs. Greenoff placed the children at her left hand, Ben nearest her, Allie toward the front of the table, and waited an instant with her hand on the back of her chair until an old lady, leaning on a woman's arm, entered and took the place opposite the children, the woman standing back of her chair to wait upon her.

"Mrs. Wiley," said the hostess, "let me present these young people to you. They are children of my cousin, Sarah Dogberry."

"Eh?" said Mrs. Wiley, lifting her wrinkled brows. "Young people, I hope you are well."

Ben and Alice opened their napkins and returned her good wishes. She was an old lady, much like the fairy god-mother in children's stories, but without that prized individual's sprightliness. She had a crook in her nose, a crook in her back, a cap which would get into steeple-shape, and a black cane; she also had very penetrating dark eyes.

"This lady is Mr. Greenoff's grandmother," explained the hostess to the children.

The door-bell rang and a few minutes afterward a young gentleman of eighteen or nineteen entered the dining-room. I say young gentleman, for, at that age, he had a full-fledged mustache and the air of a man. In appearance he was ten years Ben's senior, yet there were scarcely three years between them. He had a warm, brown complexion, and, though his head was as freshly clipt as a florist's bouquet, the black hair showed its disposition to turn into rings and waves. His temperament seemed genial, his presence magnetic. He was certainly a bright, handsome young fellow, with some polish. Alice looked

up at him steadily, and the kindly feeling flowing
from his eyes reassured her.   He spoke first to his
grandmother, bowed to the strangers, and then said
to his mother, as he took his seat:

"You must pardon my being a little late, mother.
I had some trouble getting the balance right."

"Certainly, Joslyn.   Let me introduce the children
of my cousin, Sarah Dogberry.   You never saw them,
and I confess I have not seen them since they were
quite small."

Joslyn bowed again.   A quizzical smile played
over his face at the mention of "children," and Alice could not help reflecting his smile as they looked
at one another once more.   But as for Ben, his face
flared red.   He did not mind being mentioned as a
child to the old grandmother ; but when it came to
being presented as a juvenile to a youth older than
himself only in advantages, he mentally resented it.
Mrs. Greenoff saw this and continued with ready tact,
addressing Ben and Alice while she indicated Jos-
'yn :

"And this is *my* child, very little your senior.
Your mother thought him a fine baby when last I
saw her."

The fine baby pulled his mustache and, addressing
Alice, said he thanked Cousin Sarah Dogberry for

that pretty compliment; and Alice liked him very much indeed for calling her mother Cousin Sarah. She thought, also, that if she had known Arty was safe here she would have taken more pains with her dress, and have been surer of her best hem-stitched cuffs and collar. She was afraid Ben would eat with his knife, or pour his coffee out and set his cup on the cloth, in the free-and-easy way he did at home.

That hour, a desire for refinement and refining associations as the means of the best culture, rose strongly in her. She found these strange kindred kind and genial and pleasing without any effort to *appear* so. Among the bluff New Towners she had heard polish sneered at, as a sort of insincere, social veneering which hid contemptible faults. " Still it is nicer than rudeness, even when it is shallow," thought she ; " but O ! when it goes all through, how beautiful social culture must be ! "

CHAPTER VII.

WHAT THE ELDEST DOGBERRYS DID IN SOCIETY.

MRS. WILEY said very little, but she watched the children sharply. When all rose from the table she disappeared with her servant.

"Do you like music?" asked Joslyn, turning at once to Alice.

"O, very much indeed!"

"Then let me take your brother and you to the music-room."

Allie hesitated.

"I want to go. But could you wait a moment until I run and see if my little brother is awake?"

Joslyn would readily wait. He wanted to look over the evening paper in the library; they would find him there.

With Ben creeping softly beside her, Alice ran again up-stairs. Mrs. Greenoff was required by evening callers, so they went by themselves. Nurse Tucker answered their muffled rap at the chamber door.

"Come in, dears. He's awake and has had his supper, and is just as peart and sweet as he can be."

"Arty, darling, do you know Allie? And here's brother Ben. Bless the precious!"

For answer, and to demonstrate his sweetness, the Precious lifted one little leg and kicked violently at his relatives.

"Go 'way!" he howled. "I'll *slap* ye! I'm's want my Jack!"

"Jack will come, baby. Be quiet; there's a dearie, do."

The nurse came to him with some sweet soothing mixture; and he let himself be raised, and lay propped quietly among pillows.

"He's very sore yet," said Mrs. Tucker. "A

massy it hadn't smashed his brains out, poor little love I There's the black and blue bruises on his little body would make ye cry."

" Arty, do you know Benny ? "

" No. I'm don't know ye ! "

" Darling, how did you come here ? "

Arthur closed his eyes and panted a little while. His sister's eyes filled.

" I runned off," he deigned to reply. " And 'en I called Jacky and he wouldn't come. And I cried. Big wagon runned over me — all over me. 'Ey runned on you' *dolling boy I* "

" *Poor* little darling boy ! He was hunting Jack. Where did you think Jacky was, Precious ? "

" Hiddley-giddle."

" And who brought you to Hiddley-giddle ? "

" Deedle an' Sipsey."

And that is all they learned of Arthur's journey. From hints which his memory furnished afterwards, it appeared that he had been assisted over his twelve-mile jaunt by various persons who considered him lost ; but he skillfully gave everybody the slip who interfered with his search after Jack. He talked of riding in carriages, and of big men and big wagons, but he was sure of nobody except Deedle and Sipsey.

"Will it hurt him to talk?" asked Alice, while Ben got down and made a sheep of himself to bring out a smile on the little brother's face.

" Best not to worry him, dears."

" Will he need anybody to sit with him to-night ? "

"O, no ; just his medicine reg'lar. I'll take good care of him, don't you be afraid."

" I ought to have thought of bringing clothes for him," said Alice, ruefully.

"O, don't you fret. There's lots of gowns in the house, and his little suit has been all brushed and cleaned up. It was that covered with dirt and dust! You leave him to me. I know all about children," laughed Nurse Tucker.

They thanked the good soul and still lingered a minute ; Alice to kiss the plump round of his cheek just as his eyes were closing, and, for answer, she got a smart pat from his prompt little hand.

" It's a good sign," laughed Mrs. Tucker. " Crossness, cure certain."

" I'm will kiss ye, Allie," repented Arthur. And, giving her a melting kiss, he dropped off into a deep sleep before she left the room.

Joslyn was reading in the library beside a drop-light. He showed Ben where writing materials were, with which to write a note to the children. This Ben wrote and addressed to Loo, with a plea on the outside to the postmaster to hasten its delivery; and Joslyn sent it off by Michael to catch the evening mail. Then he led them to the music-room ; an octagon with a whole ceiling of sky-light, through which, in daytime, the sunshine came tempered by the soft brown colors of the glass.

This room was still in twilight, though no burners were lighted ; and the rest of the house, not so illuminated, was quite dark. Joslyn drew some matches and touched them to what seemed to be two whole clusters of wax candles, supported by two St. Cecilias, who stood at opposite sides of an organ. Instantly the whole room sprung into great beauty. The floor was of polished oak, and the walls were wainscoted half-way up. A portrait of Mozart hung over an etagère of his music. Beethoven and Sebastian Bach also appeared above racks devoted specially to them. There were casts of the heads of Verdi and Haydn and many more wonderful men, completely fascinating to Allie when Joslyn in his enthusiasm told about them, giving sketches of their lives and descriptions of their works. There were several instruments in the room. Allie looked up with some awe at the organ with large blue pipes, built into one side of the room.

"That must have cost a considerable lot of money," remarked Ben.

"Two thousand five hundred dollars," replied Joslyn smiling, "and worth its price, every cent."

While Ben was calculating how long it would take to earn two thousand five hundred at his trade, and how much the said two thousand and five hundred would do for the children, young Greenoff picked up some rounded sticks and struck several taps on a large, flat drum.

"This is a tom-tom," said he.

Answering it, as if it were an accustomed signal, a boy entered the room through a door opposite the one leading to the front of the house, and went behind a screen at one side of the organ.

Joslyn opened the instrument and, placing his guests in seats, began playing for them. He was quite a musical amateur for one so young. Alice trembled with delight as the volume of the organ was for the first time revealed to her. She stood up and remained, like one of the St. Cecilias, wrapt in the sense of hearing. Joslyn was not a very tripping, light-fingered performer, but he had a gift for *shading* his music by combinations of stops. The enthusiasm of listeners always helped him, too; so he enjoyed a quarter of an hour of his own playing as much as Alice did. Ben stepped around the pile and took in its mechanical capacity, and watched the little blower pumping. Joslyn showed him how the bellows worked, and the effects of the stops and pedals.

" How did you ever learn it ? " cried Allie.

"O, I have just begun," said Joslyn. "I took lessons during the winter that we spent in Milan. I saw Verdi bring out his opera of 'Aida' there. It was fine, I tell you! Then I had lessons in Germany, and I practice when I have leisure. *Some day*, maybe. I can play ! "

Allie felt sure he was one of the finest performers in the country; but suppressing her conviction, she asked, timidly :

"How long did you stay in Europe? "

" We were there three or four years wandering up and down. That is, I wandered considerably with my uncle, Mr. Thorn; but mother, on Grandmother Wiley's account, stayed a great deal in Paris. My grandmother is fond of foreign countries, but does not like travel and change. She is very old."

"What is your business?" inquired Ben.

" I am learning banking with Uncle Thorn," replied Joslyn.

"I should think it was nice clean work," observed Ben.

"It is," laughed Joslyn, "when the dirty accounts don't get mixed. What's *your* work?"

"I'm a carpenter," said Ben, "and I think I'm going to like it first-rate. My notion is to get to be a master-builder, and even plan houses and other buildings. I think building is one of the most useful — and — and — important businesses in the country."

"So it is!" cried Joslyn, who loved enthusiasm in anybody. "How many children are there of you?" he added, after a pause.

"Seven. And Allie teaches; Jack is learning railroading; Loo takes care of the house; and the three little ones are growing nicely," said Ben, with family pride.

"I wish I'd found you out before," said Joslyn. "I like you. I am sure mother would have taken great interest in you if somebody had brought you under her notice; but she always has to have things put under her notice before she will attend to them. I bring the accounts of the family expenses to her and set her down to them. All women are alike," glancing quizzically at Alice, "they have no idea of the value of time, and can't account for how they spend it."

"If I had such a music-room as this," said she, " I could account for some hours I should spend."

" Don't you play ? Let me hear you."

"O, no!" Allie flushed scarlet. " She could not play, but she wanted to."

" She does," cried Ben. " She plays the organ for Sunday-school in New Town and leads the singing!"

She was then constrained to sing and she did, choosing instead of the great organ she admired, and the square piano which she was not sure of, a small cabinet organ. She sung in a sweet contralto, and Ben dutifully stood by her and roared out his Sunday bass, which, as his voice was not yet heavy, sounded uncertain in parts. Joslyn leaned against the wain-scot and watched her kindly. She really had a great deal of attraction for him.

"I should like to practice with you. It is'n't so far to New Town. Couldn't you come over some-times and learn the organ if we send?"

Simultaneously with this wonderful vista the door from the front hall was opened, and Mrs. Greenoff looked in.

"Joslyn, Professor Guilder and Rose and the McKnights are here. And Mrs. Wiley has sent down to ask you," to Ben and Alice, "if you will come to her room a little while."

"This way, please," said Mrs. Wiley's woman to the children as Joslyn followed his mother.

She led them into a hall branching from the main entrance on the ground floor, and ushered them into what seemed to be a suite divided by curtained arches. The first room was a parlor, dimly lighted, furnished in heavy old-fashioned furniture; but the second room was bright and cosy, pale buff colors predominating in it. There was a variety of easy chairs, and in the largest and most pliable of them sat Mrs. Wiley, her wrinkled hands resting on the top of her black cane and her two very small feet resting on a velvet foot-stool. She looked more than ever like the fairy god-mother, and eyed the children as they took the seats to which she motioned them as if she had half a mind to lift that ebony cane, touch each of them and change them into a Prince and Princess of the most approved fashion. She was above eighty years old and some of her faculties were impaired; but her memory and her sense of her own dignity were as fresh as when, a beautiful woman, she had life all before her as these children had.

"Wiley," said she to her attendant, "bring some bon-bons."

The woman, who had the same name as her mistress, but was unmistakably of good Irish stock, went to a rosewood cabinet, and opening it revealed its use as a cupboard of sweets. She was so neat-handed, so attentive and kind, that Allie loved her honest face. She piled three small china plates with cunning French confections of fruits, and added to each a bunch of hot-house white grapes; for this old lady had never lost her sweet tooth, and she picked daintily at her bon-bons while Ben and Alice sat before her, properly, but with great relish, tasting theirs.

"How old are you?" she asked Alice.

"Eighteen, ma'am."

"You seem a mere child. Sixty-three years ago I was eighteen. President Madison lived in the White House then, and I wore a silver tissue dress to one of his receptions. I was lighter on my feet than you, my dear. You have a pretty face." She put up her eye-glasses and, leaning forward, looked closely at Allie, the latter bearing the inspection with innocent gravity. "I want you to realize what your youth is. Enjoy it while it lasts. By and by you will be an old woman, and then you can only sit and think of the past as I do. It is a sin against God when the youth of any child is overshadowed. Are you happy?"

"O yes, ma'am!"

"Sarah Dearborn was a fair, pretty girl. I remem-

ber seeing her often with my grandson's wife. Dear,
dear ! so she has borne children and passed away.
How many did she leave ? "

" Seven, ma'am."

" Seven.   And well brought up and provided for, I
dare say."

" We are doing for ourselves, ma'am," said Ben
sturdily.   " We've been taught how to."

The old grandmother eyed him sharply and asked
Allie :

" What do you do ? "

" I teach."

" O, you instruct the other children.   That is very
pretty of you and saves expense.   I used to interest
myself in the lessons of my brothers and sisters.
They are gone, now, all gone ! Where is your watch,
my dear ? You should wear your watch and consult
it, so you can avail yourself of the best use of your
time."

Allie smiled with pure amusement.

" My watch !   Why, I never had a watch ! "

Grandmother Wiley looked at her some time before she accepted conviction of this fact.   Then,
without comment, she turned to Wiley.

" Wiley, bring me my brass-bound case."

Wiley brought a square box, very strong on the

outside, but very rich in the inside with white satin and velvet and precious stones. It shot out rainbows and vivid colors, as, placing it on her lap and applying a key, the old lady opened it. Ben and Alice could not for their lives help stooping near to look at this little Valley of Diamonds. There were two or three watches in two or three white nests, their chains meandering out. Mrs. Wiley selected a heavily enameled one with a chased "A" on the case.

"I bought this myself in Geneva, for a little girl who died. Her name was Alice, too — did I not hear your brother call you Alice? She never got her watch, so I will give it to you."

Allie drew back, though her large eyes were starting with delight.

"O, I couldn't think of taking anything so beautiful!"

"Why couldn't you?" said Mrs. Wiley sharply.

"I'm afraid I oughtn't — it's so lovely! I'm sure I never could do anything to pay you —"

"Hoity-toity! Can't I give a child a bauble? Bend your head." She dropped the long chain around the girl's neck and tucked the watch into her dress.

"Keep it to remember what an old woman has said

to you.   I suppose, sir," she added, looking up sharply at Ben, who stood grinning with amazed joy, "that you are jealous and in a rage because I didn't find a trinket for you instead of her!"

Ben's grin ran over and sounded aloud at the very idea.

"Why, I'd lots rather Allie'd have things than have 'em myself, anytime!   I think that's the prettiest thing I ever saw, and I don't know how we'll thank you!"

"You're a good boy," said Mrs. Wiley, removing her scrutiny.   "Now I will detain you no longer.   I retire very early and you will want to be among the young people."

She extended her hand to Ben, and, obeying some gracious instinct which was born in him, the boy stooped and kissed the back of it, which was like shriveled rose leaves.

"Very well, my son; I thank you for this visit," said the old grandmother, pleased by this spontaneous attention.   Then she drew Allie down and touched the girl's cheek with her lips.   Wiley showed them into the main hall, and they went along it arm in arm.

"Ben, I'm afraid I oughtn't to keep this," said Alice.

Ben harbored misgivings, but the watch was so pretty he could not in his heart bear to think Allie ought not to keep it.

"We're poor, you know, Ben, and she's — she's so kind; but she's very old, and never saw us before to-day, and Mrs. Greenoff might think —"

"Yes, so she might," said Ben ruefully. "I thought of that myself."

"I'll speak about it," concluded Alice, "and offer it back. That's sure to be the best way."

The great organ in the music-room was at this moment in a state of high musical gymnastics, and a girl's sweet soprano executing trills and crescendos.

"I'd like to speak right away," said Alice.

Still they both hesitated about re-entering the music-room where the strangers now were; so they went to the library, where Joslyn found them ten minutes later, when he rushed in for a book of musical reference. He carried them back with him and introduced them to Professor and Miss Guilder and the McKnights. The Professor was on the organ-bench, and it was Miss Guilder's voice they had heard. She was a tall blonde, very stylish, very unbending. She nodded to the two country children, continuing the remark she was making to one of the McKnights. The McKnights were cousins, Joslyn told Allie afterwards, and both of them warm admirers of Miss Guilder.

One was tall, sarcastic and exquisite, with very glittering teeth; the other a short, good-natured young man, with a voice like Punch's, and a hearty interest in every human being the world contained. The tall McKnight stood between Miss Guilder and Mrs. Greenoff, talking gracefully to both.

Allie saw there was no opportunity of speaking with her hostess, so she gratefully let the short McKnight give her a seat and turn over her opera librettos for her, and tell her in the intervals between the music, in the most genial way, as if he had known her always, his last summer's yachting experiences, and his general preference for active sports. When his tall cousin was present he was eclipsed, and Miss Guilder's presence lost to him; but he seemed to enjoy "playing second fiddle."

When the Professor began playing again, however, Allie could do nothing but watch; and as for Ben, with folded arms and eyes quite popping out, he stood by himself contemplating that spectacle with astonishment. The Professor was one of those performers who are said to "play all over." Now his shoulders galloped with his hands down the octaves, and his feet in a mad stampede thundered among the

IN THE MUSIC-ROOM.

pedals. Then he raised himself as if to leap head-long among the blue pipes and butt his brains out; but, making a quick dash to the left, he pulled out a handful of stops, jumped violently to the right as if he had made up his mind to surprise the blower at his tricks and thrash him, and only changed it in time to grab another handful of stops and climb the banks of keys again. He was improvising, Joslyn told Allie : that is, making up music as he went along. She could only wish he wouldn't.

"I think," she observed gravely, "he could find some that is prettier already written out, and it wouldn't be so hard to play — don't you?"

For reply to this innocent speech Joslyn's eyes flashed a thousand twinkles, and he went over by one of the etagères where she could see his shoulders quake, as if he were laughing to himself, and enjoying the remark to which he could make no reply.

"Professor Guilder is a great organist," murmured the short McKnight, "and Miss Guilder has a very rare voice — a pure soprano."

Miss Guilder did sing exquisitely. Her voice, un-like herself, was pliant and richly tender. For the first time in their lives Ben and Alice heard really good singing. Handel's "Angels ever bright and fair" opened a world of goodness and delight right close to their senses ; and selection after selection thrilled them with new feelings. It was in part a church rehearsal, the Professor, Miss Guilder and Joslyn, being members of a choir. Ben and Alice could have wished it to last all night, but when the callers departed they were dismayed to hear a clock in the drawing-rooms striking eleven. What hours for young folks who slept with the birds ! This reminded Allie of her watch, however, and as soon as Mrs. Greenoff had bowed the party out she approached her timidly. Joslyn was in the music-room, re-arranging his music sheets.

"We went up to see Mrs. Wiley," she began, taking the watch-chain in her thumb and finger, " and she was very kind."

" She has taken a fancy to you, I see," said Mrs. Greenoff, smiling at the chain standing out in relief against the girl's black dress.

" But I wished to ask you — " There Allie paused greatly embarrassed. When she came to do it, she found it indelicate to hint to the hostess that the elder lady might be in her dotage, and a present from her ought, perhaps, to be returned. Mrs. Greenoff understood her hesitation as delicately as she expressed it.

" Mrs. Wiley has paid you a compliment which

you must appreciate," she said heartily. " She seldom takes sudden fancies to young people. Certainly you will keep the watch, my dear. Let me see
if it agrees with mine about the time. Yes. Well, now
you will be shown to your rooms, and to-morrow I
want to have a talk with you about your mother and
all the children."

CHAPTER VIII.

IN WHICH JACK RISES AND THE TWINS FALL.

O N Monday morning Jack sat at breakfast in the cosy St. Nicholas, and opposite him sat a portly gentleman who was General Agent for the road on which J. Dogberry, the day before, made his debut as engineer. He tucked his napkin under his chin as he was the agent do, and settled down to breakfast like a man. Jack was hungry. Sunday had been a partial fast ; and in the evening after his arrival in Cincinnati, he had no appetite. He was all eyes.

The agent cut up the steak and broke his eggs, watching the boy all the time with amusement and approval.

"So you brought the train through, did you? And saved it, too! Those fellows made a wreck of some of the freights in Pontiac. I'm going to come down pretty severe on Green, the engineer you relieved, and some more of them."

"Yes, sir, they didn't act right. But I think the ones who did the damage weren't railroad boys. I don't think you ought to be too hard on them."

"You're a clannish sort of a young man."

"Well, when I'm in a business, I want to stand by the folks that employ me and the folks I'm working with. I don't believe that engineer would have acted so if he hadn't been drinking. He oughtn't to *drink*, you know."

"Certainly not."

"Our Bunch of children," pursued Jack, "sort of clan together at home. And so it comes natural to me, when I'm in a business, to stand up for it and for the other people in it!"

"How long have you been in the railroad business!" inquired the agent smiling broadly.

"Well, about two years. I sweep out the depot, and carry the messages, and take down the market reports, and do everything Mr. Joyce wants me to. I get ten dollars a month. It isn't much, but it's lots better than nothing; and then I'm learning telegraphing and all about it."

"Board yourself?"

"Yes. I board at home. I would have fifteen dollars a month; but I'm too young to carry the mails, they think, so I pay a man five dollars a month to do that. That is, they give him the money they'd give me if I could do it."

"How did you learn to run a locomotive?"

"O, I want to find out everything I can, so I'll know the whole business. I love an engine, and the engineers taught me on the road."

The agent kept smiling so Jack thought he was as pleasant a man as he had ever seen.

"So you're determined to mount the whole ladder?"

"Why, yes, sir, if I can. I think the railroad business is splendid. There's so much *git-up* about it. It keeps a man all alive, and that's the way I want to be."

"It's very lively, then, up in New Town?"

"O, course it isn't like a big city; but there are two mail trains a day and one express, besides the freights."

"I should like to see such a stirring town," said

the agent. "Perhaps I'll run up there before long."

"Do!" exclaimed Jack, "and come and have dinner at our house. We have got one of the best gardens in town; and I bet our raspberries will be ripe before anybody else's!"

"That is very tempting. Now, while I think of it, give me your full address."

He took out a pencil and memorandum book and, at Jack's dictation, wrote his name, town and state.

"Now, what else shall we order? You are my guest and I mustn't starve you."

"O, I've had a splendid breakfast, and I don't want anything more, sir."

"Well, we will meet here at two o'clock, my dinner hour. You will want to look about town. If you get tired of that, come down to the office on Vine street — next street to this, running north and south. And, by the way," concluded the agent as he took up the check and opened his pocket-book, "here is an advance on the little testimonial we intend to give you for your services. Mind, young man, I don't say I quite endorse rashness and venturesomeness; but, the way matters resulted, you saved us some money."

Jack flushed as the ten dollar bill was laid before him.

"Why, here you're giving me my meals," said he,

"and I didn't want anything for bringin' that train down. I did it just as if it had been my own, you know!"

"Yes, I know. And that's what we like. Take this now and say no more. You'll want to get some little presents for that family of yours."

Jack thought of Arty; and, putting the money with great importance and eager thanks into his porte-monnaie, he went out on the shady side of Fourth street. To a country boy the fine old street was a valley of wonders. The melancholy "Tay-tine-all-toe!" cry of the old-clothes man, the street-cars, the books and pictures and dry goods and wood-carving in the windows, the brisk boys and girls, the rush of people, the confused rumble and roar, kept him in a state of excitement which was Jack's idea of beatitude.

He went into the stores and looked at the pretty dresses — Jack had an eye for pretty dresses — and hesitated a long time over a made suit, which he had a mind to buy for Arty; but on learning that it was valued at twenty dollars he decided not to take it. Then he rambled out and found at another place a huge rocking-horse, strong enough to hold himself, and with mane and tail of real hair, and fiery nostrils and head erect. And after ascertaining that it was amply within his means, and meditating fondly for the last time on his green bill with the X's on it, he bought the horse and ordered it sent to the depot from which he was to start for home in the evening.

The spell which hangs on concentrated money being broken, Jack now acted the young prodigal and flung it about with a lavish hand. He got a pair of books for Rome and Remus, a silk handkerchief which cost exactly ninety-five cents for Benjamin, and a pair of real kid gloves apiece for Allie and Loo. Not knowing the sizes they wore, he was at a loss when the clerk asked him what numbers. But Jack was not to be balked. He described his sisters :

"Loo is tall as a tree," said he, "that is, pretty near ; and has a long slim hand. She never has had but one pair of kid gloves, but she's dreadful particular about the way they fit. Her hand sort of *gives in* and squeezes up. Allie's smaller, but it's broader across than Loo's, and her fingers don't run to such a fine point. She's had several pairs ; and I notice she gets black ones most always, but I think she'd like those pale sort of pinky-gray ones."

"The lavender ? "

"Yes, if that's what you call it. And some awful long black ones for Loo."

I may mention here that Jack came to grief on the presentation of these gloves to Loo. Allie's fitted with a nicety and a perceptible lightening of their color which delighted her heart, and she wore them with great care, keeping them in intervals of disuse in a seal-skin glove-box, presented by Joslyn Green-off. But the tips of Loo's long black gloves hung off her fingers like eagle-claws. Her slight hand roamed around in them and found no rest, and she saw, through tears of vexation, that they were sevens and a half! Jack didn't mind in the least when she ran and cuffed him with them; but declared he had described her accurately at the glove counter, and the clerk asked if she was that young person gener-ally known as the Cardiff giantess!

Disposing of his parcels around his person, Jack now wandered off up Vine street; and here he found the bronze Woman of the Fountain, standing above the esplanade and shedding from her out-stretched hands continuous sprays of blessings. He never had seen anything so beautiful. He walked all around the square to see her from every point. He approached the great fountain and examined every figure surrounding it. The child dancing by its mother's side and holding up joyful hands to catch the rain-drip from above, the boy riding the dolphin, the old man in a toga — not one piece of the groups escaped him.

"My goodness! I wish Arty and the rest could look at it! 'Twould fill all our front yard and the grove. And there she stands, winter and summer. I bet the ragged young ones like to come out and look at her. Seems as if she was mothering everybody in town. O, you pretty thing! It would spoil me to live here. I'd want to get on a rail and watch you from morning till night; and then who'd sweep out the depot, and take the market reports, and help Mr. Joyce!"

Speaking of rails made him look around to see if there were any; but the only ones to be seen were street-car rails. A little car drawn by two jaded horses came jingling along, and reminded Jack that he meant to try the street-cars and hadn't done it yet. The red vehicle stopped on a crossing and Jack bounced in. After it started it seemed to travel on elbow roads, and went just opposite the direction Jack thought he was taking. Still his bump of locality was full, and he was not afraid of getting lost. He crossed a canal bridge and the aspect of the city changed, the road grew steep; and on each side of it stood up the quaintest buildings, with galleries hung on the outside far up in the air, and nearly every name above the store doors was in German. It was the German part of the old city where good foreigners and their children keep up the good ways of Vaderlandt, and nothing is changed from generation to generation. When Jack paid his fare, with great shrewdness and business dispatch, he asked for a "round trip ticket and how far the road went?"

"Going up the incline?" inquired the conductor.

"The what?"

"Why, the inclined plane — there it is."

Jack looked in the direction indicated and saw a railroad in the air, with its terminus at the top of what seemed to his prairie-accustomed eyes a very high hill. There seemed to be a double track; and up one a black speck was sliding, and down the other came a similar black speck.

"Do folks go up and down that thing?" thought he. "I'm going to try it if the rest do." So he said "Yes, up the incline," pocketed his ticket, and watched his destination with rather a shaky heart as he neared it.

The car paused, another horse was added, and these tugged the load up to a small house, which seemed to be the "Inclined Plane" station. The full car was soon emptied and Jack followed his compan-

ions into the station, where a man tore off a coupon
from his ticket and put him into an open door which
seemed to give entrance to another street-car. A
signal sounded two or three times, then the door was
shut and locked, and Jack felt the sensation of rising in
the world. The people appeared perfectly calm ; windows were open all around. Jack crowded upon
the front platform and saw that a cable of iron wire
was drawing them up ; and down came the other car
rushing past them ! The roar of the engine on the
hill filled his ears ; and how nimbly that cable ser-
pent leaped over the revolving grooves of wood which
made its path. He grabbed his hat with both fists to
keep it from skurrying away on the wind, and wanted
to yell with delight. The great city with its mantle
of smoke drawn over its head, its spires glinting, its
river shining away to the south, rolled out below him.
Too soon was it over. The car went more slowly —
it drew up to its station — a man waiting there
clicked the door open and the people poured out.

" I've got the trip back, though," thought Jack. So
he delayed that ecstasy, wandering around the building, and looking down a circular hole at the station-
ary engine which worked the cars up and down the
" Incline." Having still a coupon of his ticket left,
he explored Mt. Auburn Street, and gazed upon its

various residences with approval ; also upon its airy height and untarnished greenness.

"This is a very fine place for women," thought Jack. "I wish all *our* girls lived in that house with the slim pillars and such a lot of porches ! Come to think, maybe they'd like this cunnin' place all over vines best. But, as for me, I like to live down in town right in the middle of everything. I don't mind the *sutt ;* but Loo and Allie would make a dreadful fuss about the washing down there."

He reached the terminus of the road and took a ticket back ; and it is a fact, which Jack was afterwards ashamed to own to his family, that he spent a long time whizzing up and down that "Incline."

When he returned to the St. Nicholas it was long past two ; but a waiter, who had evidently been set to watch for him, beckoned and placed him at a table.

Very different from his sensations, as he sat with just such a luxurious dinner before him as a boy likes, and an attentive man at his elbow to help him to what he couldn't reach, were the sensations of Rome and Remus as they fastened the front door of the Dogberry house and started off with Jacey Dixon.

Jacey lopped along, sawing from side to side in his

accustomed lazy way, his hands buried deep in his pantaloons pockets, but whether to support his pants or his hands nobody could ever decide. He never had suspenders, but tied a tow string around his waist. He was a very light-eyed youth, about the twins' age ; hollow in the chest, hollow in the temples, and very lean-limbed. He had an active imagination, and a great love for the marvelous and startling.

The three trotted down a slope which led to a deep ravine west of Old Town. As they sunk into this valley it was easy to see toward what point they were making. Here stood what had once been a tannery, a weather-beaten old frame which all the children considered " booggerish ! " not only because it looked deserted, and was full of old tan-vats into which one might fall and be drowned, but because, also, Billy Greer lived there, the terror of New Town children after dusk.

He was a rag-picker of strange habits. Bent half double, with his great sack on his back, he grovelled over New and Old Towns picking up shreds and trash. He made monthly journeys to other places, either to dispose of his pickings or add to his treasures. Danport was known to be one of his beats, the twelve intervening miles being nothing to Billy Greer. In the daytime, when he jabbered around

the gutters, many boys were rude to him, and, conse-
quently, in the dark they respected him. Billy, in
his personal appearance, was a sight that made small
children cry. He was not social, and desired to
reside undisturbed in his mansion the tannery.

"I wish the sun wouldn't shine so!" cried Maude
warm and excited, "or else that I'd brought a parasol. Why can't the sun carry an umbrella? Look
at those three or four great big clouds standing
round the sky doing nothing, when they might be
shading us!"

"I think," said Jacey solemnly, "you'd better be
thinking about your little brother down in this here
tannery!"

"What do you b'leeve Billy Greer'd do with him
if he had him?" inquired Rheem, in a voice which
betrayed his doubt of Billy's having him.

"What do I b'leeve he'd do with him? W'y, I
b'leeve he'd put him in a vat and tan him as black
as leather and then sell him!"

"But Arty'd drown!" shuddered Maude.

"And who'd he sell him to?"

"W'y, to those Italians with harps and fiddles, or
the gipsies. There was a woman came to our house
and she wanted to stay all night, and she had seven
children. Some was boys and some was girls, and

some was bigger ones! And she had a hand-cart and there was a bar'l in it. I thought they looked sort of funny ; some was light brown, and some was coffee-color, and some was purty nigh black. So in the night I heard her call them up, and I got up, too, and watched. And she'd ketch one by the hair of the head and dip him in the bar'l, and he'd come out all drippin' with somethin' like ink ; then she'd ketch another and dip *him.* The girls they cried, but the boys never said ' boo '; but one, he got his mouth full and sputtered it out, and I was squattin' right behind the bar'l and it hit me on the head. There's a black spot on my head yit. "

Jacey pulled off his cap and offered his scalp for inspection ; but there were so many black spots it was difficult to say where the dye-marked him.

" That scared me so I crept off. But next mornin' I said to the woman when she started : ' Missis, what you got in that bar'l ? ' and she says, ' Brine for pickles. I'm gatherin' pickles to sell.' And then I knew she'd stole the children and was a-colorin' them for the gipsies or Italians."

Rome's hair bristled, but Remus said :

" I don't believe that ! "

" Well, you needn't," retorted Jacey doggedly, "but I can show you the very room where the woman slept! I ain't goin' no farther. I don't want Billy Greer to know I told you he had Arty."

" When did you see him with Arty?"

" Didn't I see Arty's little linen dress stickin' out of his bundle? And last night, when I come along a-past the tannery, I heard the mournfullest noise that ever was, like somebody about Arty's size was gittin' whaled to death; and I crept up close to the house and laid my ear close to the ground, and heard old Billy trampin' round among the vats, and every little bit I could hear the licks and then a sousin' like he was dippin' the little fellow again. I bet his skin'll be so black you won't know him by this time!"

Credulous as Rome and Remus naturally were, and much as their curdling blood resented such a state of things, they could not *quite* credit all Jacey said, and halted to parley further with him, when a sound rose from the tannery which turned the burning afternoon into a nightmare. Jacey took to his heels, but the shriek which drove him drew the twins, trembling but decided, straight to the low tannery door. Remus knocked with all his might and then kicked with his boot. A humming and purring inside ceased. Remus doubled his knocks. The door opened so suddenly that he precipitated himself into the room while kicking it, and, in a wink Maude was whisked in also by the collar of her apron. The strong door banged to, and Billy Greer stood over them, like some great giant, in the twilight. It was never light in there.

"I want my little brother!" said Remus, with some little defiance left.

Billy stooped down and looked at the boy and girl. He drew his mouth around one side of his face almost to his ear; then he let go there and drew it to the other ear; then he opened it like a cavern and advanced on the cowering twins. Rome began to scream at the top of her voice; but Rheem only stepped back, turning pale, and taking care to keep his arm before his sister.

"You can't scare *me!*" he declared in a trembling tone. "You tell us where Arty is or we'll go off and raise the town!"

It seemed likely that they would go off!

The boy's defiance roused the giant of this castle to greater exhibitions of rage. He began to chop his teeth, these being large and powerful, with a regular clip which reduced even Remus to a whimper. Then he grabbed them both again and dragged them between two piles of rags he was sorting. These unfortunate children might as well have been in a

wild beast's den as in the grip of this strange
creature. He had not spoken a word to them ; but
now, as he raked a covering of boards aside with his
foot, he uttered a prolonged, triumphant yell. Rome
and Remus joined in fully, but with different feelings ; for in the earthen floor he uncoverd a tan-
vat, and they looked down into it, seeing the brown-
ish, horrid liquid about to swallow them up.

Plunge !

Rheem landed still struggling, but Maude fell
unconscious.

Why, the vat was dry! There was nothing in it
except heaps and heaps of rags, ill-smelling, but
not so choking as water. The children caught their
breath. The boards were replaced over their heads.
Billy had shut them in. They grabbed hold of each
other to be stayed and twin-supported in that dreadful place.

"Don't be scared, Rome," whispered Remus, "I
ain't going to let him do anything more with us."

Between the cracks of the boards now came a
sound more blood curdling than anything before —
of Billy cracking his jaws and grinding his teeth, and
saying unctuously — as if he could hardly wait to
finish his work before he tasted them —

"I love you ! O, I love you ! How I love you ! "

"Do you think he's chopped Arty up?" sobbed Rome under her breath.

"Po—h! No. He da'sn't!"

"But where is Arty?"

"Well, I shouldn't wonder if he threw him down here. When Jace was talkin' I didn't more than half believe he'd got Arty, but now I believe he has."

"How I love you!" gritted Billy at regular intervals, bending to the rags he sorted.

The twins grovelled among the rags in the vat. It was not a fragrant work. Dust rose and nearly stifled them; but still with the energy of desperation they poked and dug, and felt down deeper and deeper for the missing baby.

' Rheem, why doesn't he cry?"

"Like's not he's pretty near choked—this is enough to do it! Or, maybe he's asleep."

Rome put her face down among the nauseating rags and projected through them:

"Arty!"

Remus did likewise:

"Arty!"

Duet and chorus:

"Arty! you down there?"

"Say, Arty! Rheemie's here!"

"Arty, O, Arty! Arte — e – e!" in a long, cautious, whispered cry.

"I believe he *is* dead!" whimpered Maude.

"Feel and poke 'round," urged Remus, "till we hit something."

"How I love you! *How* I love you!" howled Billy.

"Rome, there's something hard down there!"

"Way under the pile? O, pull it out quick!"

"I can't get hold! I can just touch it with the end of my foot!"

"Let's make the hole bigger and go down in it."

They made the dust fly like two young war-horses, sneezed, choked, but continued to dig until Remus pulled up a box in his hands. It was not heavy, but it weighed like lead on the children's little hands, and was evidently made of very strong wood. They felt its angles and knobs, and tried without sight to estimate its size.

"'Tain't as *long* as Arty," whimpered Maude, betraying her unspoken fear.

"What are these round-headed nails on top?"

"Run your finger over 'em."

"They're letters."

"What letters?"

"I can't find out."

" Let me try."

Remus investigated thoroughly with his fingers.

" A. D. That's what they are, A. D."

At this Rome very nearly broke into a howl.

" Oh, Rheemie! A. D. stands for Arty's name;
Arty Dogberry! Oh, he's put him in here and put
his name on it!" wept Maude, with the clear and log-
ical convictions of childhood.

" O, po — h! " begun her twin though his chin was
shaking.

Outside, however, an interruption was begun which
caused them to listen with their breath in their teeth.
A heavy hand and persuasive foot was at work on
the tannery door.

" Come, I want to see you, Billy," said John
White. John White was always coming to the rescue of the Dogberry Bunch in one way or another.
This second interruption at his work made Billy
Greer so furious, he would have harmed the stock-
farmer if it were possible. He rushed out at John
shaking his fists and uttering rapid words.

" O, come, now, Billy, I know you get teased and
touzled, but you must know your friends from your
foes. Quiet down, now. All I want is the children
in here. Where did you store them?"

Doubling in his accustomed attitude, and docile

under the sane sound man's control, old Billy Greer at once conducted him between the piles of rags to the tan-vat.

" Nice roomy place you've got for your business," remarked John, glancing up the dim walls, cobwebby and smoked.

Billy removed the boards from the vat and the heads and shoulders of the terrified twins appeared.

" O, pshaw, now ! " said John with disapproval. " Tut, tut, man ! this won't do.   Don't play tricks on such little codgers.   Come, reach up, young ones."

" Make him tell where Arty is," said Rheem, when his twin and he were out of the vat.   Maude still held the lettered box under her apron.   Mr. White lifted her out by taking hold of her shoulders.   She hid behind him and carried the box, convinced strongly that she had some clue to Arty in it.

" Have you anybody else bottled under ground ? " inquired John.

Billy Greer earnestly protested that he had not. The children ran as fast as they could when they saw the daylight, and John walked out after them laughing.   They were still confused and half-smothered by the rag heap ; and Maude forgot everything but the instinct of flight, even with John White to guard the rear, until she fell up-hill and the box was brought to sight as well as memory.

"We're obliged to you, Mr. White," said Remus, dropping back with more regard for appearances. "How did you know he had us in there?"

"Jacey Dixon came tearing up to me, and told me you and your little better part had gone to Billy's to hunt for Arty, and Billy came out with an ax and cut you both in half, and was splitting you into fine kindling while he came for help."

"Well, he was pretty rough. I didn't mind much, but I hated to have him frighten Maude."

"Hold on, little Dogberry," called John as he saw Rome sprawl, "the danger's all over. I guess you two had better go home with me to Priscilla, and let her put you in the smoke-house and fumigate you with something to sweeten that pest-rag smell you got in Billy's vat."

Rome looked into John White's face as Remus helped her up. His countenance reminded one of a turnpike of granite. No down there. He was never known to wear a beard; but mica-like sparkles of fun and good-will shone over it. She thought he was the best looking and pleasantest man in town!

"If you haven't brought that box!" cried Rheem.

"What box?" asked John.

"The one we dug up in that vat. Maude's brought it with her."

Maude dared not own the secret convictions which made her bring it; so she stood trembling and wiping the dust of Billy's heap from nose, eyes and ears, with her long apron, while John White picked up the box and looked at it curiously.

CHAPTER IX.

THE GATHERING OF THE CLAN.

SOME people are always having adventures. They find what nobody else does; or they go on a journey and miss a train, to mount some delightful train of odd happenings. But Loo was not an individual to whose lot adventures fall. She really did not like unusual occurrences. So, wandering about the streets of Carver City until it was time to take the return train, she was not preyed upon or smashed; nor did she encounter any rich old rela-

LOO.

tive, who, looking upon her sweet, womanly, young face with favor, decided to make her his heiress. The only face she recognized among hundreds of strangers was that of Lawyer McKay, the Bunch's guardian.

Loo was standing outside a bookstore, looking at prints in the window, and occasionally wiping a tear off her pensive nose, when a hearty voice beside her exclaimed :

"Well, Lucy, how do *you* do ? The other children with you ?"

She looked up and gave her hand to Mr. McKay.

"No, sir. I came alone."

"Crying ? What's the matter, child ? Anything wrong at home ? Were you going to my office ?"

This gentleman was an old friend of the family. A man grizzled and brisk and talented. The first jurist in his county, and second only to the President in the eyes of the Dogberry Bunch.

It did not take him long to gather from Loo what had happened. He looked at his watch, thought a moment, and then told her he would go back home with her.

So Lucy came on the afternoon train, just as she expected to do, and with her came the guardian.

Dogberrydom stood brown and still in the evening sunshine, meditating about its emptiness. I suppose the little old house said :

"Where are all my children ? Are the boys at work ? Is sweet Alice in the school-room ? But Lucy's feet do not pat about, and I cannot see Rome and Arty on the croquet field. I don't like this. Come home, young ones! I shall die without some life in me! Why, this is a pretty way to treat your old home, that has sheltered you since you could chipper! Here's a strange cat sneaking along one of my back window sills, to find a broken pane and get into the cupboard. I don't believe I could stand this all night. I want to hear your little noses snoring. You haven't gone off to stay, have you? I'd willingly have my roof raised by a good noise; though in times past I *did* complain that you shook me considerably."

Now, to the old house's joy, Ben and Alice drove up to the fence, and, tying Thomas' sorrel, hastened up the lawn.

"Why, the door's locked, Allie!" exclaimed Ben, trying it. They felt for the key on a nail under the step (this was a family secret), and entered.

"We — ell!" breathed Alice, slowly, looking around the silent and empty place, "where are the children?"

"That's what I want to know!" cried Jack, bursting in from the station where he had just arrived. "Where's Arty? Has he been found, yet?"

"Yes, he has," said Alice, hugging Jack and shaking hands with him. "And *you're* a nice boy to get carried off while you are in bed, and travel all over the country without a clean shirt on!"

"Where have you been?" inquired the older brother, pumping Jack's hand.

Pat, pat, came a pair of shoes and a pair of boots on the steps, and Rome and Remus, with their brass-nailed box, scampered in.

"Why, here's Jack!"

"And Ben and Allie!"

"Where's Arty?"

A Babel of sounds now ensued.

"Arty is in Danport!" — "Where *you* been?" — "Billy Greer put us in a tan vat!" — "In Cincinnati!" — "Was he hurt badly?" — "No, only bruised! — He was run over! — He is at Mrs. Greenoff's! — We'll bring him home in a day or two!" — "I had a splendid time, and you can't guess what I've got for you!" — "O, I'm *so* glad the baby is safe!" "What's that box you put on the table, Maudie?" — "My gracious! what a noise! Don't; we'll raise the neighbors!" — "Seems like we'd been gone a year!" — "We've all been seekin' our fortunes!" — "Whew! Allie, where did you get that big gold chain?" — "Why, where's Loo?"

"There's a new candidate coming before this convention!" shouted John White, looking in from the stoop. "It's your *gardeen*, Lawyer McKay. Quiet down, or he might get a hickory and lick a few of you."

The Berries, now re-assembled, ran to the door and met their guardian and Lucy there.

"Any news from the baby?" he inquired directly.

With irrepressible eagerness they began all talking together again, when John White stuck his fingers in his ears and took a leap off the stoop.

"That's what I came in to ask," he cried. "I saw the horse and buggy tied down here. But you might as well go to ask the time of day of Niagara Falls!"

Ben grabbed a crayon of chalk from his pocket, and made a bulletin board of the front door, chalking out :

"ARTY

IS

FOUND!"

"Where did you find him?" inquired Mr. McKay, moving like oil among the troubled waters.

Ben and Allie related their experience.

"We sent a letter," they added, "and thought the children would know all about it by this time; but

I guess they all ran off and forgot to go to the post-office."

" Didn't Maude and Rheem stay here ? " inquired Lucy.

" I guess we *didn't !* " the twins hastened to assure their friends, " when we thought old Billy Greer had Aity, dipping him in tan-dye to make him a little gipsy ! Jacey Dixon said so ! "

" And we went right down there ! "

" And he grabbed us and put us into a hole among the rags ! "

" And he gritted his teeth and said he loved us ! "

" I bet you'd never seen *us* again, if it hadn't been for Mr. White ! "

" My goodness ! what children ! " murmured Alice. " Haven't I told you many a time not to go with Jacey Dixon, and to stay away from Billy Greer's old tan-house ? " So she embraced them, and wiped the dust off their noses.

" We'll have to go back there and take this box to Billy," said Rheem.

The lawyer picked up the box. It was of mahog- any. There was a key-hole in one side. He took a key out of his pocket and opened it. To save their lives the Bunch could not help huddling just a little nearer to see what might be in it. Mr. McKay took out one paper after another, examining them sharply as he did so.

"Where did you get this box?"

Rome, being constrained by her lawful guardian, was obliged to stand up and confess. She told why she brought it, and Rheem added to her testimony, as to where they found it.

"Well, I have taken a lucky trip, to-day!" said Lawyer McKay. "The Durand heirs have been searching for this very box, two years and a half. Whether the rag-picker stole it, or it was carelessly thrown out in his way, it is a treasure to them. Here are deeds and bonds worth thousands of dollars to the heirs. And I will see that you haven't marched on Billy and fought and suffered for nothing!"

"Mr. McKay!" cried Jack, who could keep back his own bonanza no longer, "look at that!"

Guardian looked at it. It was a cheque for a hundred dollars.

"I'd better invest it, hadn't I?" bustled Jack. "And they gave me ten more, besides. But I don't think half as much of that as I do of what the agent said about the company's promotin' me right along! And it was all for nothin', but runnin' a train when another engineer was misbehavin'!"

"These young ones does beat all!" exclaimed John White, withdrawing himself from the stoop. "You never can tell what they'll be up to, next; and throw 'em in, deep as you please, they always kick out top of the pile!"

CHAPTER X.

WHAT THE NEIGHBORS SAID ABOUT IT.

MOTHER DARLING.

NOW Mother Darling came running in, with the baby under one arm, and a pan of light biscuit, wrapped in a sweet, clean napkin, under the other. She thought, as the children had all been wandering, and in such a hurly-burly, the bread might be used up in the bin. Of course she knew Arty was found. Everybody in town knew that by this time. Mother

Thomas and the other neighboring women followed in her footsteps. You might have supposed the Bunch were their own children, they mothered them so.

John White went home about dusk, to his wife Priscilla. His farm lay a mile from the centre of New Town, and, when he was not riding or driving, he could stretch his long legs over that distance with wonderful speed. Priscilla had supper all ready. He could see it on the table through the telescope formed by the porch, the sitting-room and the dining-room. So he went around, at once, to the spring-room, where living water bubbled out of a pepper-mint-surrounded spot, and flowed away through a stone trough, and where clean towels and clean basins always abounded, and washed his hands and face ready for the evening meal. He came to the dining-room door as Priscilla emptied her hot spiced cookies from a pan, and, while he rubbed his wet hair into dry bristles, he said:

" They've found the little fellow, Priscilla."

Priscilla knew immediately whom he meant. They had no children at their house, and she was not as much interested in the Dogberrys as John; but she had a habit of knowing what John meant, every time he used pronouns referring to people whom he had not mentioned before.

"Yes, I s'posed they would find him," said Priscilla. "He wasn't hurt any way, was he?"

"Sound as a dollar, except a little bruising. They found him over at Danport with some of their old kin-folks. Seems that he ran off by himself."

"Did they bring him home?"

"No, they haven't brought him yet. But the rest are all there, yelling and prancing like so many cats. Jack's had big adventures; and the two young ones went down to Billy Greer's and hauled up some old deeds that Lawyer McKay says are worth a pile o' money."

"It isn't their money, is it?"

"No. It belongs to some heirs by the name of Durand; but I s'pose they'll get something for it, though I don't know whether they'll take it or not, the whole tribe are such independent little things. I lent Ben ten dollars to go to Danport with, and he brought back the same bills, and asked the favor of doin' a little job for nothin' for me sometime, to show his gratitude!"

"Well," said Priscilla, "sit down, and let's have supper."

About the same time, Mr. Thomas was blinking

weakly across the table at his wife, while she gave him "the particulars" of the news.

Comment by Mr. Thomas, made with a melancholy sigh:

"Well, it's better to be born lucky than rich, they say, and I s'pose them children was born lucky. *Ours* wouldn't fare that way, I know."

"Don't call it luck!" says Mother Thomas, energetically. "It's only that children without fathers and mothers is *seen to*, that's all. And I believe ours would fare just as well if we was to die — and they behaved themselves."

"Then, we'd better die," sighed Father Thomas. "They'd be better off!"

"Well, I'm goin' to mother my own as long as I can," laughed she, "and when I'm gone, then it'll be somebody else's turn."

"I think if their rich relations has lived within twelve miles of 'em ever since they came home from Yerrup, three or four years ago, and hasn't took any notice of them till now, they didn't want to see them very bad," continued Father Thomas, lucidly.

"O, pshaw, now! poor folks ain't such a takin' sight that they're to be run after. They say people live all their lives just a little ways from Niagara Falls, or the big mountains, and never go to see them, just because they can do it anytime. And 'tisn't much wonder they let relations alone that they've hardly ever seen, and take no sort of interest in. These folks seem to like the children, now that they've sort of been forced to notice them."

"The children won't get any money from that family, though."

"Well, do they *want* it?" cried Mother Thomas, impatiently. "The children are doing very well. It's better for them to take care of themselves and learn how, seeing they have to. But it won't hurt 'em to have rich friends, and to find out how the rest of the world, outside of their own town, lives."

"It'll spoil 'em."

"Well, then, they'll have to get unspoiled again, if they're so simple as that!"

Jacey Dixon, who came in the evening and jumped astride the Dogberry gate-post, and whistled the reluctant Rheem down the lawn, viewed the recent circumstances in an Oriental light; his painted fancies rising cloud-capped to the very skies.

"You got us into a pretty scrape, telling us Arty was down there!" began Remus, indignantly, as soon as he came within talking distance of the whistler.

"Yes, l sh'd think I did! I wisht I'd gone in

myself! And I *would*, too, if I'd known old Billy had a box full o' money there, savin' up for anybody that wanted it! I heard you got enough to start a bank with, and was going in partners with your other rich relations!"

"O, pshaw!" snuffed Rheem.

"Is it so, that Allie brought home a gold watch apiece for every one of you? I heard, too, that Jack was goin' to be President of the railroad, and give you all free passes for the rest of your lives."

"Who tells such things?" cried Remus.

"Well, I wish't somebody would adopt *me* and take me to Yerrup, like they say them folks in Danport is goin' to do all you! Lemmy see your watches! Hain't you got a little one you don't want?"

CHAPTER XI.

THE CATHEDRAL CHILDREN.

NE other trip was made to Danport before Arty came home. But at last he was brought in the Greenoff carriage, in Mrs. Tucker's charge and under the general guardianship of Joslyn, who was to stop a day or two with the Bunch. Mrs. Tucker went back in the carriage covered with thanks and smiles, and the Berries all clustered around their baby and their strange cousin. Joslyn examined each critically, but with sympathetic enthusiasm. Mrs. Wiley had sent her love to her favorite Allie ; his mother a note to her favorite Ben. Jack, as a young traveller, was ready to affiliate with their

134

travelled guest, and the younger children were not shy of him after they saw Arty galloping over him.

Arthur was a trifle more of a despot, being humored so much by his nurse; but he sat upon the rocking-horse Jacky brought him, and rejoiced greatly to be home once more.

Lucy and Alice got into a corner of the kitchen and consulted together after this great arrival. The outcome of their mingled wisdom was such a supper as taxed the deepest resources of Dogberrydom. As to lodging, that was easily arranged. They gave up their own room to the guest, and went up-stairs to the boys' room, while the boys adjourned to the barn.

It was another Saturday night, but the June weather suddenly changed with one of the freaks of this northern climate. The air took a cold chill; the clouds huddled together and rained a sleet-like drizzle; and at dusk a howling wind came down from the north and shook everybody's house about his ears. It was November in the heart of summer. Mother Darling, when Loo, with a shawl over her head, ran to take her the neighborly compliment of a plate of their best baking for company, bewailed her doctor's being out in such a night, for everybody else in New Town huddled in-doors.

Ben made a wood fire in the open Franklin stove, which stood in one corner of the sitting-room; and Allie pulled the muslin curtains close, resolving to send all the extra comforters out with the boys when they retired. Jack and Rome and Remus studied the brilliant Joslyn, who sat in a stuffed arm-chair before the fire with Arty on his foot. The perfume of the supper the girls were preparing came in through the mosquito netting of the kitchen-door. It was delicious comfort; yet it put Joslyn in mind of nothing he had ever experienced before. Everything was so homely, yet so — what Wiley, his grandmother's Irishwoman, would call "heartsome." The atmosphere of the house suited his spiritual lungs better than the atmosphere at home. Here were so many boys and girls, loving and needing each other so truly, yet with so little dribble of sentiment! Here were such possibilities, and such needs to develop them! Who could tell what might work out of this little brown house! The mysteries of the 'Sociation, revealed for his financial judgment, shook him with pleasant laughter. Yet he saw, in the bank of three dollars and odd cents, a great power, a sort of collar clasping into one all the Dogberry necks.

Rome and Remus brought out their corn-popper and their pop-corn; their tongues and Jack's kept popping, too. And Arthur, on Joslyn's boot, popped laboriously, but conscientiously, into the conversation, to entertain their guest with such apropos remarks as:

"Old engines go 'chug, chug, chug,' when 'ey draw trains!"

And,

"Jacky an' I feed ve *other* pigs when 'ey in the pen!"

Or else, with visions of his favorite story, "The Three Bears," floating before his mind, he dabbed out a sketch:

"An' 'ere 'ey stood with 'ey gloves on, an' 'ey par-'sols in 'ey hands, an' Big Bear says, 'Who's been eatin' my porridge!'"

"You're an odd little old gentleman, aren't you?" said Joslyn, looking down at the baby's glinting hair, big velvety eyes, and three-cornered, elfish face. "You pursue your own lines of thought undisturbed by the rest of the world. I wonder now, really, that they fitted that golden-colored wig on such an elderly person. Perhaps it was the largest one they had, however, and the only one that would stretch over that full cranium. Take it off and let us examine it," said Joslyn, bending forward and taking hold of Arty's scalp-lock.

"It's fast!" protested Arty, staring at the young gentleman.

"Humph! now don't try to impose on us. Don't you wear a wig?"

"Cousin Jos'n says I wear a wig!" said Arty, staring aside at his brothers and sisters.

"And, while you are about it," pursued Joslyn "let us examine that glass eye of yours, and these india-rubber ears that are such a fine imitation! Just look at the curves and lines of these ears. They are as natural as life!"

"My eye ain't *glass!*" protested Arty.

"You'll be claiming next that you haven't a cork leg! and that this nose of yours doesn't come off! Pull it off and let us see how it is made. Really, you are a very well put up old gentleman!"

"It doesn't come off!" asserted Arty, with bulging eyes.

"My dear old fellow! we know all about that. Your work has been done so well that two-thirds of the world suppose you are real. But — do you take yourself to pieces when you go to bed? Suppose you should get your leg on in a hurry some morning, so that the foot turned backwards instead of forwards! Why, then, one half of you would walk one way and the other half the other way, and you'd tear

yourself in two! Now that you show your teeth I
must remark that they are a very good set. The
lower ones false, too?"

"My leg doesn't come off!" cried Arty, feeling
doubtfully one of the little warm limbs which
bestrode Joslyn's boot. "You mustn't say 'at!"

"O, of course, we'll not say anything to outsiders;
but I really should like to see how you look when
you are taken apart and put in glasses of water and
hung around on pegs. It is no wonder you ran off
to hunt up Jacky, if Jacky is your valet, for you are a
helpless old gentleman without him!"

"I'll run off 'gain!" cried Arthur, beginning to
feel a personal grievance from these remarks. "I'll
let wagons run over me!"

"O, that would merely knock you into pieces, and
you'd be easily enough put together again. I do
wonder, though, at your reckless extravagance in
pegging all the way to Danport on that cork leg!
If it had worn down what must have become of
you?"

"You're real *nugly!*" said Arty, now thoroughly
on the defensive, and bristling at his teasing senior
as boy will bristle against boy.

"You're a Metempsychosis," laughed Joslyn.
Several thousand years ago you were a little trian-

gle-faced Egyptian, and you used to play hide-and-seek around the pyramids."

Arthur pondered this. His ear was sensitive to sounds, and the strange name which Joslyn called him pleased it. He told Allie when she put him to bed that he *was* a 'tempychosis; but his legs did not come off, and "Cousin Jos'n was just as nugly as nugly could be."

At the supper table Joslyn was far from ugly. He sat at Alice's right hand and helped her pass the cups, and told so many stories and jokes that the table would have been boisterous if the girls had not been such natural little ladies.

All the children sat up straight, trying to remember their best manners; and Allie's eye marked with approval that the twins — snuggling together as usual — did not smear their napkins or upset their cups, so the very best table linen might last while the guest remained.

They had a tender chicken, broiled deliciously, and Loo's best biscuit, and old Mott's butter — the finest butter of the best old cow in New Town — and mother's cut-glass fruit dish, bearing a floating island of honey in an amber sea, and cake in the old-fashioned solid basket which had been Grandmother Dearborn's, and Loo's master-pieces in

THE MAGETISM OF THE KEY-STONE.

various jellies, quivering in various lights, and chocolate — with a great deal of milk in it for the young
ones — and finally flowers — in a tall vase — seeming
almost tropical on a night when the wind screamed
around all the corners " November! " The girls
knew better than to throw these delicate and tempting dishes helter-skelter on the table, too. Their
mother, and their own observations, had trained
them to be artists, and Joslyn felt a pleasant thrill,
like that which is given by an unexpected harmony
in music, as he looked over their arrangement.

The lively young man was made — an hour afterward
— the key-stone of an arch before the crackling Franklin stove. Metempsychosis, on his rocking-horse
beside his Jacky, forming one extremity of that arch,
and Sweet Alice, fair and pleasant, the other. Rome
and Remus so owned his attraction that they
allowed him to separate them, and hung on each side
of him, and Ben Bolt and Loo sat next to them, on
either side.

The arch said they wished they could see all the
countries on the earth ; and the key-stone told them
wonderful tales about Spain, and Germany, and Pal-
estine, and England, and France, and Switzerland.
Their eyes stuck out with delight, and they leaned
forward so as almost to destroy the arch, the magnet-
ism of the key-stone was so great.

The arch then said they did wish they could hear some real good music ; and the key-stone said his head was full of music, and it sounded something like this :

"Once there was a family of seven children, and they lived in a wooden cathedral with gold pillars at the front of it. They had lovely terraces of ivory for their play-ground ; and they had also a very dear friend who frequently called them to this play-ground, and made them and himself happy with exercise. He never thought which one he loved best ;·for he could not love one without loving all, and each was different from all his brothers and sisters. If you caught one alone, you knew him from the rest of the family ; yet, at the same time, he never appeared to better advantage than when with the rest.

"Now the cathedral they lived in was a queer place, full of arches and crannies and shifting chambers. But the brothers and sisters had a lovely time in it ; and, though they did not realize it, people by the thousand — I might almost say 'an innumerable multitude' — came in front of their cathedral house to hear them as they skipped around on the ivory terraces. For, as they moved, they made harmonies. These they could not hear themselves ; but they moved according to certain laws of their nature, and as their friend led them.

" These seven cathedral children never had deep disagreements, but gave and took freely among each other ; and the friend, who delighted in playing with them on the ivory terraces, loved them more and more every day of his life. He spent days and months planning a beautiful movement for them. The more he loved them the more he.desired to make them give out deeper meanings.

" There was no jealousy among them.

" They were well united.

" They were so unlike that one was necessary to all the rest.

" But what do you think they did, when their friend brought his majestic movement for them to play ? They hid in the cathedral and eluded him, although he pulled all the door knobs and pounded at the basement. These children shrunk from what was tragic and sorrowful ; and the friend had to catch them, and pull one at a time upon the terrace, each one wailing in remonstrance.

" He felt desperately sad, and lay down with his head on the lowest of the ivory terraces. The cathedral was very still. You might have heard a mouse gnawing under the basement. The children peeped out at the front and saw, by the dim daylight, that other people beside their master were lingering in sight of the cathedral, in a restless or heart-broken way. A lady in black clothes sank down in a large space far below the cathedral and covered her face with her hands. The children could hear her cry in a smothered voice :

" 'Oh, I am dying with pain which still does not kill me ! Oh, my little baby ! your loss strangles my life ! You went out of my sight, and they say you are dead, and I must submit ! I cannot submit ! '

" 'Poor lady ! ', whispered the children in the cathedral. ' Can't we comfort her ? '

" ' What ! with some gay movement? That would never do ! '

"See that ragged little girl slipping in. How eager her face is ! What is she saying !

" 'O, I wisht and I wisht ! ' said the little girl. ' Sometimes I wisht so bad I can't stand it, but I don't know what it's for, only for better an' better ! Mebby I oughtn't to keep a wishin' for what I don't know how to come at, but somehow I can't help it ! '

" ' The poor little creature's soul is waking up and shaking itself, and looking round,' whispered one of the cathedral children. ' O, I wish we could play some movement which would fill her with joy and resolution for the rest of her life ! '

TRAGIC AND SORROWFUL.

" ' Not one of our most brilliant performances would do that. They are for diversion, for giving pleasure. The master's new movement, which we hated to learn, perhaps would have given us the key of these folks. Now there is a man gnawing his beard and folding his arms. What's wrong with him ? '

" ' The whole world is a den of selfish thieves,' muttered the man. ' Every fellow preys on his brother. Pooh ! talk about honesty, talk about love ! There is nothing but self-interest ! The human race is a very mean race — '

" ' Ah ! ' cried the cathedral children, shaking their heads. ' Nothing brilliant would put better thoughts in that man's mind ! If we knew something which would touch his heart and make it more tender ! Why, how many people there are that we can't touch because we hated to learn any painful lesson ! '

" ' Come ! what's the matter with you ? ' exclaimed a friend of the master's, approaching him. ' Call out those children you love so well.'

" ' They refuse to follow me through any sorrowful lesson,' sighed the master.

" ' What ! you, their friend ? '

" ' They have been gay and glad. It is natural for

them to remonstrate against having the sorrow of the world expressed through them.'

" ' O, try them again ! they cannot be so foolish. Do they not know they can be nothing to, and do nothing for, the human race, if they never learn its troubles ? '

" The cathedral children's friend raised up his head, and opened the doors again. Then he called with all his power to the children, and they replied to him as they had never done before. Docile and sweet and trembling with earnestness, they did his bidding. They moved on the terraces, calling one to another with a closeness of brotherhood which even the man who despised men felt keenly — like a sharp point of truth in a strong parable. They fell down with their faces on their arms, like the bereaved woman; but, above the pain passing through them, their master made them call to God who heals pain. Then they marched on, at first in blind and confusing ways, like those in which the ragged girl was lost; but a triumphal march grew out of this confusion, and at last they entered a world of such delicious harmony that words can never give it a description.

" The woman went away. The man went away. The girl went, too. But the cathedral children had spoken deep things which were never to be forgotten, to these three, and perhaps to many more. The pillars of their great dwelling glittered dimly in the night, and they slept. The gates were shut upon the ivory terraces, and even their friend was gone. But wiser and stronger for having felt and borne part of the woe of the world the seven lay silent in the cathedral ; and the echoes of that movement will stay there as long as the seven children do."

"Well, that's an odd story!" remarked Jack, when Joslyn stopped speaking.

"Tell 'Three Bears,'" suggested Arthur, fixing on an entertainment more to his mind.

"It's something about the seven notes in music,' said Allie, hesitating.

"You get it!" laughed Joslyn.

"And it somehow seems," she added, "to mean us seven children, too."

"We never had a knock-down fight in our lives!" cried Jack. "We get along pretty well together!"

"But when we grow up and have troubles," murmured Loo, " I wonder how we'll get along ? "

"I tell you, now, I *would* hate to see any of the girls come to grief!" cried Ben, who understood Joslyn's fiction as a parable, " whether they ought to enjoy it alongside of other folks or not."

"O, *I'd* stand by *you*, Rome!" cried Remus.

"And *I'd* stand by *you!*" she responded.

And "I'd stand by you!" "I'd stand by you!" resounded all along the arch.

Before they knew what they were doing, the Bunch were all standing by each other and shaking hands with each other, reassuringly.

"O, we'd all stand by each other," said Allie, laughing, "and if by each other by everybody else who needed it!"

"You *are* a Bunch!" said Joslyn, rising also and laughing and shaking himself. "Well, hang close! But it's nearly twelve o'clock, and I believe my further hints and admonitions to you now will have to be curtailed with 'Good-night, Dogberry Bunch!'"

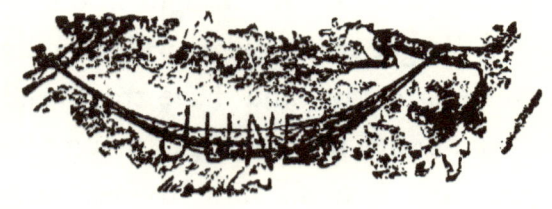

CHAPTER XII.

"NO HOME!"

IT is a fact in our existence that some days or weeks, crowded with events, seem longer and of more importance than months or even years of quiet living. During the years, however, we are growing ready to burst into the flower of new events.

For two years after Arthur's journey the Dogberrys went on pretty much as usual; on a new plane to be sure, and improving themselves, but without any important adventures.

The Greenoff family did not forget them. Joslyn gave Alice music lessons, and the whole Bunch, in instalments of two or three berries at a time, were taken to visit in Danport. But Allie's every-day life was one of school work and planning out the children's clothes.

The Durand heirs were so glad to get their brass-bound coffer that they very readily sent the twin discoverers of it a couple of hundred dollars apiece; and this great property Rome and Remus solemnly turned over to their guardian to be invested at ten per cent, along with Jack's hundred. They felt that they were mighty capitalists. In seven years, if the interest remained untouched, their fortune would double. Their heads often swam with considering how they might use it to the best advantage in life. On first coming into their estate they proposed dividing it equally among the family; but all the Bunch except themselves scouted the very idea. Now they were thrust into the enviable position of heirs! and Rheem never met Jacey Dixon anywhere without taking care to act with humility, for fear that highly imaginative boy should think he was proud.

During this time they thought much about enlarg

ing their house. Their tastes and ideas were growing. So Ben and Alice took tithes from their earnings, and Jack and the twins turned over their two
years' interest to the fund, and Ben himself built a
wing, raised the roof of the summer kitchen, and finished the latter room with a rough plaster. They
had now a parlor, a dining-room and a kitchen, a
guest-room and two roomy chambers for themselves.
There was so much consultation and so much waiting before these rooms could all be furnished and
arranged according to their satisfaction, that it was
quite six months after the beginning that they got to
the outside of the house. It needed a new coat of
paint, and they all went out and looked at its brown
and weather-beaten sides.

" Let's paint it white," said Jack.

O, no ! Allie couldn't endure white.

" And white lead costs like fun," said Benjamin.

" And a white house always looks like a big tent,"
said Lucy.

" I think green would be pretty," suggested
Rheem. " I never saw a green house ! "

" And you're never likely to see one," said Jack ;
" especially Dogberrys' house. When I was in Cincinnati —" Jack was very fond of soaring back
through his travels — " I noticed a good many nice
buildings painted gray and brown."

"In stripes and crossbars, eh?" quizzed Ben.

"No, I don't mean *that* way. I mean some were brown and some were gray. Gray's a pretty color."

They held many councils, and Ben Bolt investigated every shade of pigment. A very pale brown was found to be as cheap and pretty as anything they could command. Pale brown it was, and Ben, in putting it on, emphasized it with darker facings. Under this treatment the old house appeared actually to expand. How fine, warm-toned and hospitable it looked!

"There's one thing more," said Sweet Alice, "but we can't afford it! That's a verandah."

"I tell you what looks nicer," cried Rome, "and that's these stripey covers cousin Greenoffs have on their windows."

"Awnings."

"They'd cost as much as a verandah," objected Lucy.

Still their minds all ran on that subject. The house stood back on a well kept and shaded lawn, and the awnings would be more delightful than verandahs all around. So they thought and inquired and planned, and finally made for themselves some wonderful cheap awnings, with covers to go under when it rained, and ropes to pull them up, and a framework satisfactory in the extreme.

"JUST PRETTY ENOUGH FOR ANYTHING."

Then they sat down on the lawn and looked at their house quite half a day. It was a beautiful place. It looked like a sea-side cottage. None of them had ever seen a sea-side cottage, so this simile did not occur to them ; but they pronounced it with one accord " just pretty enough for anything ! "

Arthur, in knickerbockers and blouse, and his first boots, and a straw hat so broad that it quenched him like an umbrella, looked solemnly at his rejuvenated home.

Mother Thomas, going home with her sewing under her arm, from spending the afternoon with a neighbor, saw the group camping and came up to find what they were about.

" Why, how fine we are ! " exclaimed she. " Got your house done ? "

" Clear finished ! And O, isn't it sweet ! " cried Rome. " I'm so glad we got everything just fixed in the summer time when the trees are green. I'd feel sorry if it had to stand out in the snow when it looks so new ! "

" We're sitting here taking our leisure to admire it because we've been so long about the work," said Sweet Alice, smiling. " We've been nearly two years planning it all and raising the money to fix the house. Haven't we, children ? "

" That's because girls are so full of notions and so slow," cried Jack. " If we'd been all boys we'd had it done long ago ! "

" Yes, and what a sight it would have been," said Lucy. " A whittling place, a sleeping place and an eating place, and all doors so's you could run in and out easy. That's a *boy's* house ! "

" Now, Loo ! " remonstrated Ben," this is part a boy's work, and you seem to think it's pretty credit-able."   .

" It's first-rate ! " said Mother Thomas, shaking with good-humored approval of all that the Bunch did.

" But you ought to see the new rooms ! " cried the twins.

" And the kitchen ! " cried Arthur.

" And the china closet ! " said Allie. " O, you must come in and see it all ! "

So they took her amongst them — some pulling and some pushing her, the tall ones calling her attention upward, and the short ones bespeaking her attention downward — and showed her first what improve-ments they had made in the sitting-room, the band of dull Indian red at the top of the wall, a case of books on a table, given them by Joslyn Greenoff, their attempts at " applied art " on some cheap bits of pottery, and the effect the awnings produced in the room. Then they dragged her to the wing-room, fresh and new, the wood grained dark by Ben's untrained but really imitative hand, the chamber set the best their hoarded means could buy, the grand easy-chair, put together of rough wood by Ben and covered and stuffed by the girls; then into the closet pantry which their budding architect brother had introduced between the dining-room and kitchen, with a window where the dishes could be handed back and forth, and with such shelves! and such snug locker arrangements with lids, for bread, cake, etc.

Last of all Mother Thomas was constrained to view the glories of the new kitchen, raised from its former low estate of shed; and, though she had previously seen all these things piecemeal, not one but many times, she expressed as much astonishment and joy over the completed whole as if her eyes had never before rested on a moderately comfortable house.

"Stay to tea with us," begged Lucy, who, having done her week's baking, felt sure of a tolerable bill of fare.

"Yes, do!" urged all the Bunch, when a shadow pushed over the door-step and across the parlor floor and quite into the dining-room, where they were almost clamoring in their eagerness and joy.

"There's some one at the door. Maybe it's Cousin Joslyn!" exclaimed Jack.

They made a charge on Cousin Joslyn, but it was their guardian, Lawyer McKay. He was a welcome comer, too; though they were all just in tune with Joslyn's happy nature at that moment, and would have loved, of all things, his criticism or approval of their work.

Mr. McKay had to go over the whole round which Mother Thomas had just finished. They asked his opinion of the wing, and desired to know if he didn't highly admire the band of Indian red under the parlor ceiling.

"We'd like to put a new carpet in the parlor," said Allie, "but we can wait for that."

"Yes, till after we have bought an organ!" cried the twins.

"And some more books," said Ben.

"And some pictures!" exclaimed Jack. "What does a fellow care for carpets? I just as lief tumble down on the bare floor, if I can have something pretty overhead to look at. These pictures that mother made at school are real nice, but they make a fellow want more."

Sweet Alice observed that their guardian viewed their improvements with a grave and clouded face. She and Ben Bolt as the heads of the family felt their responsibility. She did not wish him to think they had been indulging in prodigal expenses.

"We put a rug carpet in the new room," she observed, calling his attention to it. "It didn't take nearly as much carpeting as if we had covered the floor; and is so much prettier with the border! I bought that with the money I meant to get a new summer suit with, but I didn't really need the suit as much as we needed the carpet. Ben made that stain for the floor-border. When you see how little it cost us to make these changes, Mr. McKay, you'll be surprised!"

"It's very pretty," said guardian.

Lucy, while the others were acting as ushers, had touched up a quick fire in the kitchen stove and set the kettle to boil. She now rolled out the table, put in an extra leaf, and they heard her rattling with much importance in the new china closet.

"I did all the carpenter work myself," said Ben, "and got the lumber at the lowest figure — and the paints, too. There's a good deal in getting your materials cheap."

"You're an energetic, bright lot," said Lawyer

McKay. Still he appeared no less troubled than before.

" We just used the interest of our money," observed Jack, with importance, "and some more that we earned and saved on purpose."

" And now we've got lots of room !" cried Remus.

" Plenties ! " cried Rome.

" Just as pretty a home as anybody need want !" wound up Jack.

"They do enjoy anything so much!" remarked Mother Thomas to the lawyer, shaking her portly figure with sympathetic laughter.

" You've used the interest of your money," said Mr. McKay, queerly, "and have been putting your spare earnings into these improvements ? "

" Yes, sir !" chorused the Bunch with faint apprehension.

" We thought you were willing we should go ahead and make them, sir," said Ben.

" I was.   At the time it seemed the wisest investment you could make."

" My gracious !" thought Mother Thomas ; " if the man has any fault to find, why doesn't he out with it instead of talking so scary — just when they're taking such comfort in everything ! "

" And — wasn't it the wisest investment ? " inquired

the Bunch, all of them turning up their eyes on him, solemnly — except Ben, who stood on a level with his guardian and, therefore, looked straight at him. Arthur's straw hat was pushed to the back of his head — he was the baby still, and manners were not rigidly enforced on him — his hair straggled down to his eyebrows, his immense, serious eyes were spread wide, to take in the full measure of some calamity which Mr. McKay appeared to hold over their heads.

"No," said their guardian, slowly. "If I had known then what I know now, I never should have advised it. I should have been very far from allowing you to put your means upon the house. I am afraid you are going to have trouble, children."

A breathless waiting for the worst.

"There is another claimant to this property."

The younger ones scarcely understood.

"Another party has a title to it."

"That won't do him much good, I guess!" exclaimed Jack, hotly. "Our father left this house and two lots to *us !*"

"But it seems there was a flaw in your father's title."

"Didn't you think it was all right, Mr. McKay ?" asked Alice, piteously, very pale about the mouth.

"Of course I thought it was all right !" exclaimed guardian. "I never examined into the title very closely; but White, after he had settled up your father's property, turned over the papers to me and told me you had your home and your lots. The taxes have been paid regularly — "

"I'm going to Mr. White this minute," said Jack, "and ask him if anybody owns our house and lots but ourselves !"

He darted across lots for John White's.

"White was appointed administrator, you know," said Mr. McKay. "I was appointed guardian. He is a good and honest man. I suppose he knows nothing about any irregularity in the title, and such a thing never occurred to me until I got a letter yesterday setting forth a valid claim of another party, and demanding possession."

"Possession !" gasped the Bunch — except Arthur, whose eyes expanded more, if possible, and drank in whole draughts of the doleful tidings.

Lucy, drawn from tea preparations, stood leaning disconsolately against the dining-room door-frame.

"Sit down, Mr. McKay," said Allie, faintly, realizing that she wanted very much to sit down herself. Ben wheeled the large chair towards him and he sat down, looking really distressed among his wards. Alice sat down and took Arthur on her lap. Mother Thomas, who had a constitutional distrust of law and lawyers, also entrenched herself in a chair, and prepared to support the children through the danger now threatening them. Rome and Remus interlaced arms and firmly propped one another. Ben took a stand similar to Lucy's, and leaned with one brawny arm above his head.

"If father bought and paid for this property, Mr. McKay," said he, "and got all the papers for it, isn't it ours?"

"If the papers are right," replied guardian; "if he made his title good. There are very many instances of defective titles; and a piece of real estate will change hands again and again, the lawyers never finding out that another party has the rightful claim till that party turns up to make his claim good. I suppose you might have gone on comfortably all your lives in this house — some of you — if a certain man hadn't left his affairs, when he died, in the hands of a very sharp person. That person now claims this little piece for the estate, on the grounds of an informality in the first purchase."

The Bunch were mystified but greatly distressed.

"Nothing but a quit-claim from these original own· ers could make your title perfect."

"Couldn't we buy a quit-claim, then?" Ben begged to know.

Mr. McKay shook his head.

"Everything depends on what they may choose to do."

"It's a shame," cried Rheem, "if our father paid out his money for our house and other folks can go and take it from us!"

"It's just as bad as can be!" assented Maude, crying. "It's stealin' things!"

"It's unfortunate," said guardian, "truly. But the law doesn't rob, and, especially, doesn't rob orphans. We'll see what we can do."

John White now entered with Jack panting at his heels, and, after gravely exchanging greetings with Mr. McKay, asked to have the case repeated to him. The two men went into the guest-room — alas, that its first use should be such a funeral-like one! — and held a consultation. John White had administered on the very small Dogberry estate, and had done it to the best of his ability. He had seen an abstract of the lots and considered everything safe.

"Do you think they'd better fight this?" he asked, greatly disturbed. "If they haven't the means for it, I have. I feel like I ought to see the thing through." John's granite-like face showed the quartz and feld-spar now, instead of its usual mica-like glints of fun.

"Frankly, no," said their guardian. "There's a minor on the other side, too. They'd get involved in endless suits, or get judgment against them ; for the thing's very clear. I wouldn't have had this happen for a year's income ! "

"It's a shame ! " cried John, "discouraging the little tribe so, when they're so full of hope ! More energy than half the grown folks — and just got their house fixed up to their idee ! "

"There's this," said Lawyer McKay, indicating a point on which to fasten hope. "The Dalrymple estate is very large. This is a stray bit of one of Dalrymple's investments in Western lands. In this locality it isn't very valuable to the estate. If there wasn't a minor heir on that side, too, I might get a quit-claim deed from that estate which would make these children safe."

While their friends were conferring the Bunch huddled together in the parlor. Mother Thomas secretly indignant at being shut from a consultation in which she felt a vital interest, went home, pained and excited over the probable fate of the children, and they remained for some time without speaking.

Then Sweet Alice, unable longer to bear the strain of controlling herself, wiped two oozing tears from her eyes and murmured :

"What *shall* we do if we have to lose our home?"
The twins took up the wail:

"O – oo – oh! No home!"

And Arthur emphasized it by opening his mouth even wider than his eyes, and joining the melancholy chorus with a whoop of grief:

"No-o home!"

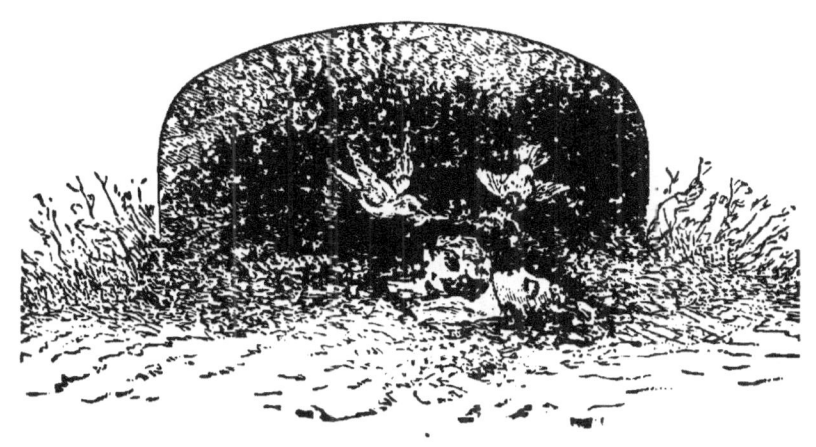

CHAPTER XIII.

BLACK SHORT-HAND.

AFTER his short consultation with John White Mr. McKay went home again. He paused at the door to cheer them up as well as he could.

"At any rate you have possession," said he, "and will keep it until the matter is settled one way or the other. We'll do the best we can."

John White walked to the railroad station with him, quite roused and anxious.

How different their house looked to them now!

They got up and marched over it again. They lamented in the spare room. They regretted the beauty and finish of the china closet. In their wrath and desolation they wished they could say "Abracadabra!" and turn the kitchen back into a shed!

"That lovely band of Indian red!" said Lucy.

"Our awnings!" exclaimed Rome and Remus, tremulously. "We'll take them off — so we will! We'll carry them away with us!"

"But where shall we carry them to?" said Allie. She and Ben gazed at each other.

"Well, don't let's cry till we're hurt," urged Jack. "Mr. McKay says we've got possession and can keep it till we're turned out; and if they go to turn us out we'll shut the doors and windows, and — and — and — yes, we'll *fight* 'em!"

Jack saw an imaginary host of big harsh men armed with clubs and true titles, and his soul rose in resistance.

"There's no use in our talking," said Ben — as the Head of the House he stated plainly their position to them all — "if we have to give up our home we'll just do it, and get another the best way we can. Perhaps the time's coming for us to stand by each other!"

They drew closer together.

" There's our four hundred," exclaimed Rome.

" You can have *all* that," said Remus.

" Yes, we'll have a little left," observed Jack, " for there's *my* hundred, too."

Sunday passed dolefully. On Monday Allie went to school as usual. Ben put in a good day's work on one of the buildings which were habitually rising in New Town. Jack did his station business, and Loo kept the home machinery running. But in them all there was a secret solemn looking towards the impending crisis. At four o'clock Rome and Remus came home from school with Arty toddling between them. He deserted them near the station and went to his Jack ; and they went straight to the loft over the stable to carry out some literary work which they had planned.

This loft had no windows except broad chinks between the boards ; but they considered it a delightful sort of studio. For ceiling it had the brown and pointed roof ; and the swallows, like low murmuring musical-boxes, played continually under its eaves. The floor was very clean. There were two stools, and a table made of a box set on legs, with a lid which raised, disclosing treasures of copy-book fragments and bits of blank paper torn off letters. In

one corner — and convenient to the studio, like an
Italian apartment — was Maude's own special private residence, her cupboard preserving all the
dishes ever broken in Dogberrydom ; her table,
made by Remus, and slightly uneven-legged like a
kangaroo, and both her rag and china dollies.
Raggy, with oblong head and stiff crosspieces of
arms and her pencilled features half defaced, lay
sprawling out in her blue calico, looking very much
discouraged ; but the China, whose charming name
was Helen Evelyn Rosalie Dogberry, sat up in a little rustic chair made of roots, and kept house beauti-
fully.

"Susan," said Maude to Raggie, "you do look
ridiculous poutin' down there. I'd switch her if I
had the heart, for showing such a disposition ; for I
set her up straight at noon and this morning, too,
and she kicks over every time. But maybe she feels
bad about us going to lose our place, and doesn't know
what in the world *she'll* do for a home ! "

"Maybe she's sick," said Rheem, beginning to
search his breeches' pockets for a stub of a lead pencil, taking out a bunch of string, some flints, three
paper birds, a half-shelled ear of corn, two knives
(one swapped and to be delivered up the following
morning for a jews-harp, which the other boy forgot

to bring that day), some nails, and a small padlock and key, and half a dozen matches.

"Let me have my key," said Rome, "maybe she is sick. I'll unlock my house and see."

She very gravely received the padlock and key just mentioned from her brother's hand, and, stepping to an imaginary door rattled the two together.

"Lock, lock, lock, lock! Now it's open. Susan, what's the matter with you, my sweet child? Aren't you well? Or have you lain down on the floor just to show your naughty temper? Look at Helen Evelyn sitting there like a little lady!"

Here she changed her voice to a tiny plaintive whine and spoke for Susan.

"Ma, she won't let me have the chair at all! She sits in it all the time, and I have to stand up or lean across one of the cupboard shelves!"

"What, Helen Evelyn, won't you let Sister Susy sit in the chair? You mustn't be selfish with your sister!"

"Yes, ma, Susy may have it."

"That's a good girl! I guess you can both sit in it. Now kiss each other."

She bumped their faces together. Helen Evelyn's nose appeared worn away somewhat by greetings of a similar character on harder substances than sister Susy's cheeks. And she had lost one foot, but did all that she could genteelly to cover that defect. The foot had wandered to school in her ma's pocket. Maude meant to sew it on again — it being a china foot on a cloth joint — but, in an unguarded moment, she traded it off to another girl for some chewing gum, which Allie prohibited her chewing. So it was a dead loss; for the girl wouldn't trade back, and Helen was injured for life. Perhaps this circumstance made her heart tenderer towards this doll, for all the handsomest clothes fell to Helen ; but favoritism did not spoil her sweet disposition.

Having crowded her two children into the root chair, Maude drew up the table before them and gave them a bit of wholesome and nourishing candy for their supper, with a great many bits of broken china from the cupboard shelves for them to feast their eyes upon. Susan was still slightly perverse and stuck one foot upon the table, declaring that Helen Evelyn squeezed her out of the seat; but her mother checked her with a reproachful shake of the head.

"Come on," said Remus, "I've found it!" producing from a fold of his pocket, where several fish-hooks were embedded, a speck of lead pencil to which he carefully gave a point, and in doing so reduced its size so much that it wabbled on the paper between his finger and thumb.

"I must put 'em to bed first."

"O, let them put themselves to bed! We'll never get our letter done."

Rome took her key and, retreating, again made magic passes with it.

"Lock — lock, lock — lock! Now the door's locked. Here, put up the key for me, Rheemie." Then she returned to their sanctum and studio.

Remus was already on a stool with the fairest half sheet of paper before him, sucking the lead pencil stump. He took the key absently and slid it into his trousers' pocket.

"Now, don't lose it," exhorted Maude, in her usual formula; "for what 'ud I do if those children should be locked in, and their clothes should take fire and I couldn't get to them!"

"I won't *lose* it!" cried Remus, spurning the idea, as he always did, though his daily path was sown with lost doll-house keys, and he had once been obliged to force the invisible door with a corn-cob that Maude might get in to her starving dollies. She now brought her stool close to his, and put her arm around the back of his little vest.

"Do you spell dear with a big D or a little d?" inquired he.

"Big," said Maude.

He wrote laboriously. "Dear — "

"Maudie, how does Cousin Joslyn spell his name?"

"I don't know. I'll run and ask the girls."

"Don't you!" cried Remus, bringing her down in full flight. "We weren't going to tell! We were going to write our own selves!"

The truth was that they instinctively knew the family pride would keep the older ones from pouring the tale of Dogberry calamity into Joslyn's bosom. But no such pride hindered them, and they did not want to be hindered by anything else. Joslyn was a mighty power in their eyes. His fertile nature had often added to their joys. It was now the very luxury of trouble to display it before him. What he would do they did not know. Something tremendous, probably. One thing they were sure of, and that was his warm — his real comforting sympathy.

"Well, how do you think it's spelled?"

"Don't write it. Put a J and wait till we get through; then maybe we can think of the rest."

"Dear J. —"

"Say Mr. McKay came and told us we hadn't got any house or lots."

"How do you spell McKay? I wish there wasn't so many names! I guess I'll put it K — 'n' then we can fix it. 'Dear J —, K. says we haven't any

property ' — that sounds better than lots.   Property.
Le's see.   P-r-o-p — ''

   " P-i, pi, proppi — ''

   " Aw, pshaw ! don't le's say property, it's so long.

" LE'S SEE.   P-R-O-P — ''

Le's say residence — that's what folks call their
houses.   R-e-z, res — ''

   " R-e-*s*, Rheemie ! Don't you know how to spell
residence ? ''

"O, I can *spell* it; but it takes so long to write, and this pencil slips so! I'll put it R."

"Little r, or else we'll think it's somebody's name when we come to read it over."

"'Dear J —, K. says we haven't any r.' Then I'll say 'We feel very bad.'"

"Yes, write that; and put in 'All of us do — awful — even Metempsychosis!' He'll know we mean Arty, for that's what he calls Arty."

Remus wrestled along until he came to Metempsychosis. Then he and Maude gazed at each other, and without a word he put it M.

"Tell him 'We would love to see you and the other relations.'"

The spelling-shirk was now chronic. When Remus came to "relations" he made another phonetic character, and his work got pretty rapidly down the page. Maude would have taken a turn at the pencil, but Rheem imagined himself the better scribe, and told her they better not waste any writing-paper on her experiments; for they might soon be driven into the world without a scrap. Submitting to his decision she contented herself with prompting him.

They poured forth their souls and made a very expressive letter in intention; and then they tried to translate it out of the original.

"Read it over and hear how it sounds, Rheemie."

"'Dear J —: K. says we haven't any r. We feel very bad, all of us do, awful, even M. We would Love to see you and the other R. There is something wrong with our t. Somebody else has better t. We might get a c, but there is a young h. You ought to see our house. It is r and has A at all the windows. If we have to leave it we shall feel d. The dolls are well. Loo broke a g and I was glad to have it in my playhouse. I caught sixteen fish the last time I went. We got good bait in our garden.

Your loving C,

RHEEM DOGBERRY, }
MAUDE DOGBERRY. }

"I get all mixed up!" cried Rheem, puckering his soft eyebrows at his twin. "I forget what some o' the letters stand for!"

"J, that's Joslyn; and K, that's McKay; and r that's —"

"We've got in *three* r's!"

"Well, r stood for relations once, I remember."

"We haven't any relations! Now that ain't right, for we were going to tell him something about the house. And down here it says: 'You ought to see our house. It is r.' Now *that* ain't relations. Our house ain't our relations!"

"That was repaired; and then it has A, you know — awnings!"

"O, yes! 'There is something wrong with our t —'"

"Title —"

"It sounds mighty queer, doesn't it? 'If we have to leave it we shall feel d —' dreadfully. 'Loo broke a g —' goblet. I saw her break it. But we've got the fish and the dolls mixed. 'Your loving cousins.' We'll have to study over this and find out how to spell the words before we send it, or Cousin Joslyn won't know what we mean."

"We can hunt the words in the big dictionary, I tell you, Rheemie," proposed this devoted sister. "I can run and bring it out here now!"

"No," cried Remus, "I'll put the letter in my jacket pocket, and we'll hunt the words when the rest of them go out to sit in the Air Castle or play croquet."

"And to-morrow we'll get a stamp and envelope and send our letter."

The business of the studio was now finished, and they climbed down the ladder and went to the house.

But they never sent that short-hand letter to Joslyn. When Jack came to supper he brought the mail, two letters; one addressed to Allie, the other to Ben. Allie broke her envelope first and read aloud :

" MY CHARMING COUSIN AND THE WHOLE BUNCH :
I write in a hurry to say that we are off to the Arkan-
sas Hot Springs, almost without warning. My
grandmother, Mrs. Wiley, has been failing greatly.
The physician thinks the baths and the climate may
do her good. Of course mother goes with her, and
Wiley (Mrs. Wiley's woman) with them. And they
imagine there is something the matter with me,
though I cannot be convinced of it myself ; but as
they need me to look after them, and I haven't had
any vacation from the bank for an age, I shall go and
get as fat as the heat will let me.

" The house will be shut up, probably for the
whole summer ; for if Mrs. Wiley can bear it we
shall take her from place to place. We are really
very much alarmed about her. She is quite old, and
her life has to be very carefully guarded. She was
delighted with that white shawl you netted for her,
Allie, and sends her kindest remembrances, in which
mother joins. ' Bless you, my children ! ' Be good,
all of you. I should love to rush in among you
before we start ; but we start to-morrow, early, and I
have everything to attend to. Will write again.

With loads of appreciation,

" COUSIN JOSLYN."

" Poor dear old lady ! " said Allie.

But Rome and Remus looked at each other in a consternation peculiarly their own. How should they reach Cousin Joslyn with a letter if he was starting out to caper all over the country?

Ben broke his envelope, and his troubled face over his letter stopped any comment which would have been made upon the first one.

"Out with it, Ben Bolt," said Jack, stoutly. "That's Mr. McKay's office envelope. Have we got to tumble out?"

Ben handed the letter over to Jack, who read it with a ring as if he defied its terrors.

Guardian had another message from the party claiming their lots. The ground was wanted to build a grain elevator upon. The claim would certainly be enforced, and the ground taken possession of as soon as the law allowed.

"A grain elevator!"

"On our ground!"

"Maybe right in front of the house!"

"What is an elevator?" cried Rome, between her sobs.

"Why it's what they go up and down-stairs in when they don't want to walk," explained Remus, just as tearfully. "I saw one in the hotel at Danport."

"We don't want any nelevator!" said Arty, very

red and white with his emotions. " We won't have it! We'll tear't down ! "

" It isn't that kind of an elevator, Rheemie," explained Ben, with a husk to his voice. " It's a

" WE'LL TEAR 'T DOWN ! "

high building to store grain in. And there isn't any use in our making a fuss."

The girls tried to staunch their eyes, and Remus flung away five or six tears with his finger tips.

"I tell you what le's do," said Jack. "We've got our house done. We enjoyed fixin' it, and put our money and time on it. Now le's have some good out of it! You never can tell what's going to happen, do your best. So le's have one royal good time to remember!"

CHAPTER XIV.

RED SHORT-HAND.

THIS philosophy struck kindred sparks in the rest of the family, and they at once prepared to have a good time.

The supper dishes were soon on their shelves, and the house as trim as a new schooner. Then they made another procession to look at all their improvements, and rejoiced over everything, Jack declaring

he was glad after all that they had such a nice looking place to leave.

"It's more credit to us than the old house, and
whoever lives in it will feel obliged to us."

"It's a *home*," said Allie. "The next people can't
help knowing that."

For fear this subject should grow moister, they ran
out on the lawn and trooped up and down over
every familiar spot. Rome and Remus swarmed up
into the Air Castle, and Arty bruised his shins trying
to follow. Loo put a pansy band all around his hat.
Then they all played croquet, till it grew so dark
the balls were hopelessly hid by the grass, and then
they brought chairs out, and cuddled in them or on
the stoop, close together. Loo had some spice cookies in the pantry. She brought them out, and they
munched and were happy. By mutual understanding they let their future alone, and told stories, and
jokes, and rhymes. A freight train rumbled past.
and they watched through the trees the glare of its
eye, and a solitary figure or two darting back and
forth on it.

"No. 8," said Jack, with business address, lifting
Arty up on his knees to watch it. If there was one
thing on earth more attractive to Arty than locomotive power, he had not yet discovered it. He stood

on Jack's legs, bracing himself by Jack's scalp, and strained his eyes till the freight was quite lost in darkress, and even its two ruby rear lamps were obscured. Then he slid to his feet, and sat down again on the step, murmuring:

"The Big Black Horse!"

"Say 'The Big Black Horse, Arty!'" cried Rheem.

"Can't say it."

"O yes, you can!" said Jack. "We've said it a hundred times. Cousin Joslyn won't make you any more poetry if you go and forget it."

Arthur wriggled on the step and professed himself able to say "pieces" of it, if Jacky would do it, too. Jacky, therefore, darted off like a mother-bird luring her young one to fly, and Arty flopped alongside as well as he could, very glib with some of the lines and making a mere mumble of the others. In this way they had really recited "The Big Black Horse" a hundred times, thereby greatly edifying their family.

"The Big Black Horse is my heart's delight,
I run to watch him by day or night.
I waked in the night and I heard his hoofs
Come making thunder past walls and roofs.
He snorted coals, and they flew up higher
Than even the glare of his eye of fire.
He panted and rushed and my breath I hushed —

How awful to be by his tramping crushed ! —
The houses shook as his carts flew past,
All barred and darkened except the last.
A rose-red light hung over its dash
Perhaps so the driver could see to lash
Any hangers-on, who might love to crash
Through dark — through cities—through water-course,
   At the heels of the glorious
     BIG
     BLACK
     HORSE!

" The Big Black Horse wears a brazen bell,
In towns and at crossings he rings it well —
' Get out of my way, little sons of men,
The Big Black Horse must go by again ! '
Burnished and clean is his panting hide;
You can see a bright throb dart along his side !
He often draws carriages, long and fine ;
So strong is he, I have seen a line
Of five or six follow in his course.
He can draw *lots* of people — can that black horse !
He isn't afraid of a narrow road !
Just give him a foothold, he'll pull his load.
But pit-falls have caught him as fierce he strode !
Then people have cried over many a corse !
   But *I* should cry, too, for the
     BIG
     BLACK
     HORSE !

" The Big Black Horse gives a ringing neigh
When the curb is put on him his speed to stay.
His mane is a lovely, changeable roll,
Gray, brown, pearl-color, or black as coal !
He tosses it back and it streams out grand,

You can see it curl far across the land.
And when I am tired, and want to go
To seek more places than those I know,
And to think as fast as his mane can flow,
He says: 'Come on, I will take you so!'
He drinks from a cistern built on stilts,
And the man who feeds him, he almost wilts !
For he is a creature of fire and force —
            Ah, *how* I love him !— that
                BIG
                BLACK
                HORSE !"

After "The Big Black Horse" they proposed a story — not exactly a serial, but still a story, handed from one to another "to be continued." This was a favorite Dogberry amusement, and often afforded them a great amount of fun ; and one imagination stimulated another, though each story-teller gave the tale the twist of his own peculiar genius.

"You begin it, Jack."

" Let Allie begin this time. She's the oldest. And let's go this time in the order of our ages."

"Pitch in, Sweet Alice."

"'Pitch in' is slang, Rheemie."

"Well, then, walk up to your crib ! "

" That's a great deal worse ! Those things are not manly. They sound like the Bee Hive people."

" Well, you know what I mean. Start the ball !

Give her a send! It won't come our turn for ever so long, Rome. We can be making it up to piece on."

"Start up, Allie."

After being exhorted thus several times, Allie started up with :

"Once there was an old woman who was bent half double, and she was very, very old. She lived in a large city, in a beautiful house, and had many people to wait on her. She had three orphan grand-children whom she was educating, and they gave her more delight than anything else, when they were good and tried to learn kind manners and lovely ways. The eldest and youngest were boys, named John and Jacob, and the second was a girl, named Mary."

("What ugly names!" murmured Rome. "When it comes my turn, I'm going to change them!")

"John was tall and studious, Jacob was chubby and playful, and Mary was very graceful and very fond of music. She would sit at her piano hours, singing and practicing difficult studies; and it was her greatest desire to go abroad and study music with the foreign people who know it so well. 'When I am a grown woman,' she would say, 'if grandma will let me, I will get my big brother to take me, and we will travel and study. It would be so lovely, too, to stay month after month in Milan and learn the Italian method.' Then —" said Allie, whose forte was not story-telling, wishing to cut short her introduction — "go on, Ben."

Ben came up to the work with little relish, but perfect good-nature, and rubbed his temples with his knuckles to stir up his brain.

"O, yes! Well, one day the good old grandmother was taken very ill and died.

which straightened her out, you know. The three children felt very badly — "

("That's just as mean as mean can be!" cried Rome. "I was going to have her take them to a beautiful ride and make a picnic for them. But then — I can make her come alive again!"

"Keep still, Rome," urged her twin.)

"They felt very badly," continued Ben, "and they felt worse, when the crossest and sharpest relation they had in the world came to live with them. This aunt made Johnny take his drawings and his wood-carving out of his own room into the attic, where he had no room at all among the old lumber. She would not allow Mary to practice because the piano hurt her head, and little Jacob soon became lean because she dieted him so strictly. But John studied away, for he wanted to become a first-class architect and builder; and he often said to himself: 'When I am a man, and am making money and getting a fine reputation, I will take my brother and sister to live with me and leave Aunt Nettle to complain herself to a shadow. I'll build a handsome house of rough gray stone. No basement. Six rooms on the ground floor, but only three on the upper floor besides the passage. One for Mary's music-room, one for Jacob's play-room, and one for my work-room.' Go ahead, Jack."

"He didn't build his house anywhere except in his head, did he? Well, one day John got very mad, and concluded he wouldn't stand it any longer, so he took his sister by the hand and Jacob under his arm and started for the train. He left them on the depot platform and went in to buy tickets, and when he came out his brother and sister were gone, so he was obliged to start out on his travels by himself. He felt very badly, and concluded to go to California to make a fortune, after which he could hunt the others up and build that house for them. But when he got to California he found that the fortunes had all been made and a good many of them lost, and he jumped on a ship to go to China, but the ship was wrecked on one of the Cannibal Islands, which the missionaries have never reached. The cannibals killed and cooked all the fat passengers, but put John in a coop to feed, and he thanked his aunt whose worrying had kept him thin. While the cannibals were trying to put flesh on him, his brother and sister were in a strange city, for they had gone off on the wrong train, and their aunt was hunting for them all ; go on, Loo."

"My gracious ! John in the Cannibal Islands, and

his brother and sister away off in a city the other side of the world.   Well, the cannibals ate him up — "

("No — o " cried the twins.)

— "And Mary found a place to work, and kept her younger brother with her and sent him to school. At first she made dreadful bread and forgot to put the sugar in her cookies, and got scolded. And Jacob tore his clothes, and she never could keep his heels in ; but it was so nice to try and keep people comfortable, that after awhile she got on very well, though she often sighed to see her brother that the cannibals had eaten — but she didn't know that.   I don't believe I can think of anything now.   Oh, yes : one day her aunt happened to come to visit at the very house where Mary was, and as soon as she saw her, she took Mary and Jacob by the ears and led them off home ! "

"Ho, pshaw !" said Rheem, taking up the thread, discontentedly.   "Le's see.   One night John woke up — "

"In the cannibals ? "

"No ! he didn't get eaten ; that was a make-believe, like they have in stories : they had him just cooked ready — I mean just ready to cook — when something scared them, and they put him up again.   And one night he waked up while they were all asleep, and

took a boat and slipped off. He rowed back to the
town he started from, and looked all over the depot
for his brother and sister, and his aunt happened to
get off the train with them then, so he found them,
and she found him and took him home and shut him
in the garret. He concluded he would fix up the
garret and live there; so he made a whittling place
in one corner and built a play-house for his sister. I
thought of a lot more, but I've forgot it!"

"And one day his grandma came up-stairs," began
Rome eagerly, "and told the children to come down;
their aunt was gone home."

"But the grandma was dead!"

"Oh, *that* was just a make-believe, like they print
in stories. So they came down, and she had them
all dressed up in their pretty clothes, and took a
lovely basket of lunch and called the carriage, and
they all started off for a picnic. They came to green
woods where the grass was soft and thick — "

("What a refreshing sight to John after the Cannibal Islands!")

"And *Clarence* — his name wasn't 'John' a bit!
—said, 'O grandma, I will always be good hereafter!'
And the others said they would. And they had an
elegant time. Go on, Arty.'"

"An' 'en," said Arty, after hanging back a

moment, "they got on train, and they rode and they went and they rode and they went, and it sounded 'cling! cling! cling!' an' they never got off any more at all!"

"So John, and Jacob and Mary are still moving!" laughed Alice. "Well, children, we must move too. It's time to go to bed."

Still they lingered a little while, lapsing into silence. One of them presently

struck up the "Home of the Soul." Amuse themselves as they might their thoughts came back to
home ; they sung it heartily. And before separating
for the night they were moved by an unusual impulse : they kissed each other all round, and shook
hands, half laughing and merry, but still with tears
in their eyes.

So, having had one more good time they went to
bed and to sleep. Arty still slept in his long crib in
the girls' room. Maude, also, had a small bed to
herself.

In the night Allie dreamed she was choking.
Some tall being with wings, or a mass of heavy
drapery, settled down on her neck and began to press
her breath out. She struggled and woke to find her
nightmare continuing. She was smothering ; the room
was full of smoke. She sat up dazed and unable to
think. The open window was obscured, though when
they went to bed there was moonlight. Color now
came out in the smoke. It bloomed suddenly, and a
fearful roaring and crackling filled the whole house.

She was helpless and speechless ! It seemed ages
before she could raise her hand and lay it on Loo.
Her voice sounded down in her chest and horribly
hoarse and strange when she could utter :

"Loo, the house is on fire ! "

Loo sat bolt upright, and said, "What is it?"

Then the truth bursting upon her, she uttered piercing screams and sprang to the floor; it crackled beneath her feet. She pulled at Maude, and snatching Arthur up ran to the door with him in her arms. At the opening of the door, jets of fire burst through their carpet, swept up the window-casings and ate up the light curtains like a flash.

"Maudie," said Alice, hoarsely, snatching the child, and wrapping the bed-spread around her and dragging her shoes on, "run — run for your life, while I wake the boys!" She took the water-pitcher and dashed water on the child's head as she started, and rushed out herself, still carrying it in one hand, panic-stricken. The boys' room was near the head of the stairs. There were but two rooms and one long, narrow hall on the second floor. The hall was now a furnace. Alice ran, covering her head and face, and stormed at the boys' door. The floor was parching her tender feet. She poured out the water on them and dashed the pitcher against the door. Ben's and Jack's voices were in clamor. They dashed out, dragging Rheem with them and shouting "The girls!"

"Girls! girls! The house is a-fire!"

"They're all out, boys! Run! run!"

"Come on, Allie —"

Their voices all died in a choking gurgle. Creeping close to the ground they got down the stifling stairway. The closet under it was roaring like a furnace. But they all reached air and ran into the dewy grass. The roof was one mighty blaze. Distant cries were beginning to ring through the village of "Fire! fire!" Men with pails came running and scaling the fences; but the well was in the kitchen. There were no hose, no fire-engines, and sheets of flame were waving out of the very windows.

"Where's Arty?" was Jack's exclamation.

"Loo brought him out in her arms," cried Alice. "There are Maude and Rheem, and there's Loo!

"The barn's burnt!" exclaimed Ben in consternation, watching the falling timbers of that little pile "that must have set fire to the house."

"Loo, where's Arty?" cried Jack, again.

"Why, he's right here by me. No, he isn't. Arty! where is he? I just put him down. He's gone to Allie. Arty!"

Jack darted to Allie, and screamed in her ear "Do you know where Arty is?"

Allie screamed back over the terrible roar and crackle, "He's safe — he's with Loo, I told you!"

"He isn't! I bet he's left in the house!

"Loo brought him down first one, Jack!"

Jack, panic-struck for his pet brother, dashed into the house and made for the stairs. He had on his trousers and boots, but nothing to protect his head; and Allie who knew his desperate courage, was wild with despair. She felt fully assured that Arthur was safe, but nothing could convince Jack of that at this moment. She seized one of the men by the arm and pointed after her brother, screaming that he was going up-stairs again — he would be burned to death! The man shouted to Jack, and ran up and down shouting to others — and the roof fell in.

Allie ran. She flew to the farthest part of the lawn, and fell on her face in the wet grass, shaking with paroxysms of sobs and cries. Jack was dead! Dear Jack was killed! How could she ever look up again! An unsteady rustle through the sweet clover, a whispering beside her, and a hand on her neck made her conscious that Arty was beside her, but she hardly noticed him. Loo and the twins were screaming near the falling house, and she heard Ben's hoarse, despairing cry of "Jack! Jack!"

O Jack, Jack, the dearest, the manliest boy! How could they live with Jack gone! The timbers gave another crash, and sparks streamed away up to the zenith.

Arty rustled off again, howling with distress and

terror. The child was in such a fright that he had hidden himself. The glare showed him Loo, hanging with her face down on her arm against a tree, and the twins crying in their night-clothes beside her. He toddled to them, and just then Ben and two of the men came carrying something between them.

"The jump stunned him," said John White.

"Water — quick!" cried Mr. Thomas.

"O Jacky," cried Arty, "what's the matter, Jacky?" He fell down at Jack's feet and hugged his legs with loud lamentations.

The rest of the family were around him in an instant, but even in the strong glare of the fire they could not recognize him. His hair was burnt off, his face blistered as if it were half roasted — no eye lashes, no eyebrows left.

Dr. Darling knelt down by him. Allie took his head on her shoulder. The doctor gave him restoratives, and covered him with wet cloths. "Afraid he's swallowed fire," said he, and immediately made him swallow something else.

"He jumped out o' the back window," said Mr. Thomas, with a melancholy shake. "The roof nigh about caught him, but I guess he was pretty well charred, anyhow."

One side of the house swayed and fell in, sending

up another long stream of sparkles.   Nobody noticed it.   The Bunch's fate of homelessness was quickly written out — written in flame-red short-hand.   But they paid no attention to that : they stood around Jack.

CHAPTER XV.

TRIBULATION.

WHEN Jack raised his puffed eyelids and blinked at his brethren and sisters, the first thing his groping hand touched was Arty's head.

"Arty!" he gurgled.

"Jacky!" howled Arty.

"I thought you were in the fire!" said Jack, with a freer breath. Arty would have thrown himself on Jack's neck, but was held back. Jack, however, reached after him.

"Where is he? I heard him speak, but I can't see him. I guess something's the matter with my eyes!" said Jack, with a short chuckle.

"Something's the matter with your whole face and head," wailed Loo, the twins joining her in a chorus of "ah — hoo — hoo!" "You've got all your hair burnt off, and you're blistered to a crisp!"

"You dear boy," murmured Allie, "why did you run in the house again when I told you Arty was safe?"

"Don't know," said Jack, grinning with agony. "To enjoy it as long as possible, I guess. Is it burnt down?"

"Can't you see it's all one heap of flames, and the walls all fallen in but that one on the north side?"

"I can't see anything. Am I blind, doctor?" asked Jack, feeling the doctor's whiskers and spectacles.

"We'll try to keep you so for awhile," replied Dr. Darling, fastening bandages on his head, crosswise and up and down, until his nose and mouth were the only samples of it visible. Mrs. Darling, who had brought the bandages, stood near by, comforting Rome and Remus. Rome still trailed the counterpane like an Indian princess. Rheem had on his hat and boots and a long night shirt. Ben was nearly dressed ; but Allie did not know how scantily she was attired until a neighbor wrapped her in a long shawl. And as for Loo, she stood weeping and trembling in somebody's coat.

"You can walk, now, can't you, Jack, boy?" asked the doctor.

Of course he could. He reached out and they lifted him up. Raising his boots high in the air and plunging dizzily he showed them how well he could walk.

"Still, you won't mind my keeping one arm around you, will you, deary?" said Alice.

The doctor took his arm on the other side, and Arty towed him in front by one of his broken suspenders.

"We'll take him right over to our house," said the doctor, "and Arty and you must come with him."

"Loo and Ben will go to my house," said Mother Thomas, grabbing them both with determined hands. " Poor young ones, how you look ! Though, for that matter, I haven't got on much more myself ! "

"I'll take these chickens," said John White, appropriating Rome and Remus. "Bub's got his boots on, and I'll carry the girl."

"But I want to see how Jack is all the time,"

wailed Maude, hanging to one of John's big fingers.

" O, you may come and see him all day to-morrow, after Priscilla gets a stitch of clothes on you."

" Children," called Jack, painfully, to all the separating Bunch, " we had one more good time, didn't we ? But we've given up the house sooner than we expected to ! "

Mr. Thomas was heard growling at a little distance what a shame it was that orphan children should be used so, and if there was law worth calling law it would give them their lots, anyhow.

" They needn't have given possession till fall, though, if the worst come to worst," said White.

" O, let 'em go ahead with their elevator, now," laughed Jack, who had to be very merry and chuckle a great deal to keep from groaning.

" Isn't this yours ? " asked a boy, thrusting something into Alice's hand as she moved off with Jack. It was her watch and chain. She always slept with it under her pillow, and instinctively grasped it in one hand as soon as she waked Loo. It had fallen in the grass after she got outside.

" 'Thank you, dear. Yes, it's mine. Here's my watch, Jack. That's saved."

" Good ! " said Jack. " Doesn't it seem funny, though, that the band of Indian red (oo–oo !), and the china closet, and the new bed-room furniture (oo–oo !), and all our duds, and the swings and the books aren't anywhere at all ? "

" Don't cry," comforted John White, picking up Maude and her trail. "I'll get ye home to Priscilla, presently, and then you must go to bed and stop chattering your teeth and shaking."

"Helen and Susan are burnt, too !" shuddered Maude. "Everything is burnt up. I didn't know last night that I'd never see them again ! "

"I wonder what started the fire !" speculated John, as he stretched long steps over the ground.

" I had some matches in the stable. Six, I guess," confessed Rheem.

"You young scamp, did you ? "

" But we never struck any ! "

"You dropped them around, and something set them off. Maybe you stepped on 'em yourself and lighted 'em, and never noticed it."

" And the root chair," Rome added to her inventory, "and the table and cupboard ! And I haven't any dolls ! "

The dismal little pair before the end of another half hour were put to bed by Priscilla, and about morning they fell asleep.

It was ten o'clock when Rome woke from her

sleep of nervous exhaustion. She was in one of Priscilla's spare bed-rooms, on a great feather-bed, which had the peculiar smell of all its class to such a degree, that the faint sweet scent of the rose-embalmed sheets could not take it away. The wall was covered with a greenish paper, its ornament being a vine, the leaf whereof was the size of a sunflower, but was evidently a pumpkin leaf. And some of Priscilla's best dresses hung from nails above the head of the bed. The room was so small that Maude felt squeezed in it. A flowering shrub shaded the window, and the low reaching arms of the apple trees thrust themselves against the panes. There was a bowl and pitcher on the wash-stand, but when Rome slid to the floor she found no water in them. Neither had she any garments with which to make her toilet. She slipped out barefoot and in her nightgown into the keeping-room.

Priscilla was a Yankee woman, and all the New England ways of a past generation which she learned from her mother and grandmother were carefully and thriftily preserved in her clean shaded house. In this room there was a fire-place, carefully scoured, and black and gilt chairs, with roses on their straight backs, placed in lines along the wall.

In one corner stood a huge clock, with a case big

"SETH THOMAS."

enough to hide two or three children in, weights like sledges, and iron hands. The Arabic figures made a circle on its yellow face, and O, how slow it talked!

"Tick"—a time for due deliberation, and then, forcibly—"tock!" No hurry. None of the clicketty-clack of modern clocks. It looked like a giant. Maude considered how flat it could crush her by dropping a weight upon her, and what a real iron rod one of its iron hands could prove. All of a sudden it began to rattle as if it would certainly choke to death, and never catch its breath again while time lasted, and then it struck!—struck? It banged! It beat ten awful strokes into her head, and she jumped from the floor at every stroke, her black-lashed eyes blinking and her blonde head dodging. And then the old monster settled down as if nothing had happened, or ever would happen again, and said : "Tick"—deliberation — "tock!" and kept on saying it with increasing solemnity.

O, what a clock! She saw the name "Seth Thomas" printed on its face, and it became an object of greater fear on account of having a name. For, of course, Seth Thomas was the clock's name, or why should it be printed there. The name sounded strong when she timidly tried it on her ears, and it sounded unbending. Besides Seth Thomas, there were in this impressive room two pots of paper roses, one on each corner of the mantel, and two small silhouette pictures on the wall, of a sharp-nosed lady in a cap and a turn-up nosed gentleman with a high shirt collar, and a long settee without any rockers.

Maude was so afraid Seth Thomas might make some other demonstration, even more frightful than

his choking, that, clad as she was, she dared not lin-
ger here, but ventured to open the door into the
dining-room. Through this she saw Rheem washing
potatoes out on a porch, in a pair of Mr. White's
trousers hanging to his toes, though they were rolled
up until they were as bunchy as a Turk's, and in one
of Mr. White's linen coats which swept the ground.

"Here you are!" said Priscilla, briskly, coming
out of the spring-room with her hands full of fruit
for pies. "Go into the spring-room and wash, and
I'll bring you some clothes."

Maude patted across the floor, and found towels
and abundant water, and peppermint stalks in the
water, which gave it extra virtue in her eyes. The
destitute child took her bath, and dressed her tan-
gled hair with a comb which her hostess provided.
She had shoes, for Allie put them on her at the last
moment before they ran from the burning building.
Priscilla came in presently with an overskirt of her
own, and a long calico sacque which made the child
look like a dwarf woman, all waist and arms.

"There's your breakfast," said Mrs. White, pointing to the warming oven; and in it Maude found
some lovely toast and broiled chicken. She also had
a mug of milk and a sweet roll. It was a breakfast
to make an orphan forget her troubles. After eating

it she went and sat down by Rheem. He had his
potatoes washed. These he carried to Priscilla, who
was in the full tide of putting on the dinner to cook,
and then he sat down to take counsel with his twin.

"Rheem," she exclaimed, "le's start right straight
off to see how Jack is!"

He glanced down at his apparel and said, reluctantly:

"Don't you think we better wait till about dusk?"

"O, no! What if Jack was dead!"

"Jack won't die. He and Ben got their clothes
on. I wish I'd got mine on."

"Rheemie, what we going to do for clothes to
wear?"

"I guess we better go to work and earn some,
right off."

"But we can't work in borrowed things."

"Maybe Mr. and Mrs. White would fix some
things for us, and let us pay for them working afterwards."

"And never go to school any more? And ne'er
see Ben and Allie and Jack and Arty and Loo?"

"Na — w! Just till we can get something to wear.
Then Mr. McKay will tell us what we must all do.
I'm going to ask Mr. White to hire me as soon as he
comes in from work."

Rome endorsed her twin's plans as she usually did. He followed the fieldward road to the men, and she turned all her energies to assisting Mrs. White. She laid the table and did many little errands. I have said Priscilla was not as fond of children as her husband. She was a taciturn woman, kind mainly, but not winning. She .scarcely spoke to Maude all the morning, although she felt great compassion for the child. Her mind was taken up with her work. She was planning ahead the churning, the preserving, the baking.

At half-past eleven, sharp, Maude was allowed to ring the iron bell hanging on a forked post in the back yard ; and, in prompt response to it, the men and horses trooped into the barn-yard. By that time Rome was really tired. She had been so anxious to please, and taken so many unnecessary journeys, and stood so much on her feet, in dread of Priscilla's disapproval if she sat down, that she was quite tired. At table, among the jolly and voracious farm hands, Remus broached his proposition to work for board and clothes, and John laughed heartily and patted him on the back.

" We'll see about that," said he. " This afternoon I am going to drive into town. You and sis can go along and take a look at the rest of them."

This the two children gladly did. Maude's costume was heightened by a grave black straw hat of Priscilla's, entirely too large for her. But everybody was so compassionate over the burnt-out Bunch that she found her attire only heightened the interest of her position.

Jack said he was doing royally; but his blistered face was terrible, and his eyes had been dressed and bandaged again. Allie had been in the school-room, Arty with her. To lose a day was to lose some fraction of her salary, and she dared lose nothing. She looked very well in Mother Darling's clothes. Much better than Loo in Mother Thomas'; for, Mother Thomas being portly and Loo very slight, she was obliged to overlap and girdle in, and still go about looking quite like a timid giraffe in an elephant skin. Ben had also been at work, but the Bunch now convened for council. Mother Darling's babies (she had babies in every stage of infancy) rolled about among them, and crowed or squalled or uttered irresistible fragments of speech. Mother Darling herself was even more charming than when surrounded only by her own army. She winnowed the babies out and kindly left the children to talk by themselves. Some of the older babies picked up some of the younger ones, and struggled along like cats carrying kittens. All of them were chubby, and all in miraculously-kept fresh white clothes.

The dazed Bunch, huddling up to Jack's settee, didn't know what to do.

" We can't stay as we are another day," said Ben. " I must rent a house and put you into it."

" I wonder if Mr. Joyce will give anybody else my place ? " hinted Jack, anxiously.

" I wish I had a dress," murmured Rome, feeling a vague dread of Mrs. White's personality enveloping her within that awful basque and overskirt.

They were all unusually still and got hold of each other's hands. It was almost a Quaker meeting, after all. Off their own domains, uprooted and flung one side like weeds, the Dogberrys were somewhat wilted.

When they separated again — after one of Mother Darling's exquisite teas, which they tasted sparingly, for the former young householders were feeling themselves a burden on the community — it was agreed that Ben should summon them to their next meeting as soon as anything definite was decided upon.

Rome and Remus went home with Mr. White, and both of them with lumps in their throat. It seemed ages ago that their house was burnt. Everybody had got used to it. They felt lost in a boundless sea of homelessness. They missed the cheerful stir of home when John set them down in the shady orchard before driving into the barnyard. Frogs were uttering lonesome cries, and all the summer insects, from the shrill cicada to the musquito, filled the air with minor chords.   To crown all, a whippoorwill sat in the orchard and jerked out his doleful exhortation, until Maude's heart swelled to a mountain of heavy throbbing flesh.   Priscilla had all her work done ; even the milking pails washed and turned upside down on the garden palings.   She sat on the back porch busily stoning fruit for the next day's canning. Her impassive features looked so stolid that Rome sat down very meek and quiet on the lowest step, and Rheem was still and meditative one or two steps above her.   They felt quite burnt out and bereft of every tie on earth.   Ah, the songs, the scamperings, the cheer of Dogberrydom !

" Le's play 'Hi tally O,' " said Remus, sturdily. And then he remembered that two would make a scanty fox hunt.

" Have you a croquet set, Mrs. White ? " he asked.

" No.   We don't have time for such nonsense."

This was a witherer.   Were all royal good times nonsense ?

"I believe I'll go to the barn," said Remus. His twin skipped up and patted along beside him. They were humbled and aimless, and snubbed by fate and depressed. When they reached the barn John was gone to a far off pasture to feed stock.

Before the last red streaks faded out of the sky all the White family retired. Remus went again to a bed in the corner of the immense long room, where the hired men's joking jarred his sore little heart a long time before they went to sleep, and their snoring his weary ear when they did finally drop off.

In the green-vined feather-bed closet Rome lay listening to Seth Thomas. How awful he was! Nothing else sounded through her silence and desolation except his "tick!"— and then he kept her breath suspended and her eyes strained — "tock!" If Loo were there, or Allie, or if she could put out her hand and touch Arty in his crib! What if somebody should come there in the night and carry her off! How easily anyone could climb off the ground into her window! She said her prayers, begging fervently that she might not feel afraid any more; but, whether her faith was weak or her nerves strained, she was almost as much afraid as before. Then Seth Thomas was taken with his hourly fit, and rattled and banged nine fearful bangs, and she could not, for her life, help trembling lest he might walk his wonder boots right in at her, and stand glaring down with those awful eyes into which they put the key when they wound him up.

CHAPTER XVI.

DESPERATION.

THE next day it rained, and Ben did not come. The day after it rained harder. It was only a mile to the center of New Town, but none of the White household had any errand there, and no message came out to the twins. The third day it had got in the habit of raining and kept on the rest of the week. Mr. White was obliged to go away on a business errand, which he called " looking up stock."

If the house was somewhat drear when lighted by his hale and genial presence, what was it with him gone, and the rain over it like a jailer! Rome felt that she could actually gallop five times the distance which separated Rheem and her from the rest of the family; but how dare she undertake such a feat in Priscilla's borrowed clothes — through the rain?

Never before had these two children felt the actual galling restrictions of poverty. Their outlook was bad enough, but their present was terribly wounding to their delicacy and native independence. They overheard Priscilla remark in her unruffled and terse way, that she didn't like to have children around underfoot! Underfoot! They, late householders, and actual heirs to a cash fortune! This fortune now began to look large in their eyes. They consulted about it in whispers, in the porch corners, or cuddling in the prim sitting room together. They were still mindful of their characters as guests and tried to show appreciation of such kindness as was given them; for they had entertained, and knew how heavy on the hands a sullen or dissatisfied visitor is. But every day they seemed to sink deeper into the position of little dependents and pensioners. Neither could have analyzed the feeling, but both were depressed to the last degree by it.

The sun was in time obliged to shine out once more, and he came most gloriously when he did come. It was a crystal morning, trembling drops hanging on every point; the grass so fresh that every blade seemed just born; the air so clear that every object was cut out with distinct edges in it; the larks and wood thrushes singing as if they would lilt their souls out and die in the next gush. Rome and Remus were so glad they slipped down the front lane and jumped like colts. New Town roofs and walls were plainly visible, and Rome and Remus climbed upon the garden palings looking in that beloved direction, with some hope that now the clouds would roll off their prospects, too. They saw a figure plodding across the wet fields towards them, and the air magnified so that Rheem was sure it was Ben. They watched it like two forlorn, but spirited mariners on a rock in mid-ocean, and waved their hands to the sail coming to their rescue. The sail waved back, and even sent them distant halloos. When it got a little nearer they found it was Jacey Dixon, with his pants girded as usual at the waist, but turned up in the legs until his knobby and bespattered knees poked out. Jacey slouched up, and they felt more enthusiasm at seeing him than he ever before roused in them.

" How do you do, Jace ? Did Ben send you ? "

" No, I guess he *didn't !* " replied Jace, myste-
iously, grinning vacantly at them. Rheem was on
top of the fence with his legs through the palings.
Rome was poised like a hen, but suspended flying,
and even her own breath, to hear Jacey.

" Are they well ? " she cried.

" I *guess* so," replied Jacey.   " All but Jack — and
you knew about him."

" No we didn't.   We haven't seen any of the children since Tuesday.   It's rained so, you know."

" Are you going to stay here always ? "

" *No !* " cried Rome, with sharp energy. She
couldn't bear to think of such a thing.

" What you goin' to do, then ? "

" Why, we're waiting till Ben comes for us.   Then,
we're going *home !* "

" Yes, we're going *home !* " said Maude.

" Ho ! " said Jacey.

" Did anyone send you out here ? " asked Remus.

" No.   I just come myself.   When I saw the others goin' off I wondered if they was runnin' away to
leave you."

" What you mean ? " cried the twins.

" Why, didn't you know they've all gone off ? "

" *Who's* gone off ? "

" Your folks. They went on this morning's train."

" You're just a-storying."

" Mebby I am ! I guess I seen 'em, though. I like to know what *you're* going to do, now."

" Jace Dixon, you tell us what you mean by saying the rest have gone off and left us ! "

" I don't mean nothin'. I saw 'em get on the train. And I heard you two was out here, and I wondered if they was leavin' you here to get shut o' ye ! "

" Oh — hoo ! " wailed Maude, breaking into passionate sobs and tears. " But Jack isn't gone, I know. He was all blistered in the fire, and the doctor had his eyes fastened up ! "

" Yes he is, too," said Jacey with solemn triumph. " Two or three people led him. He's gone blind in his eyes. Stone blind ! I heard the neighbors say he was goin' to Chicago to have his eyes ampitated."

" He isn't blind ! " cried Rheem, with vain resistance.

" He is, too," said Jacey. " Blinder'n a fish-worm. He can't work no more, and he'll have to go the poor-house."

" He won't, either ! I guess we've got money and we'll give him that ! "

" You needn't feel so big. I guess you haven't !

The rest is goin' to git all you've got and take it with them, to buy clothes and things with ; for Jack's hundred dollars won't more'n pay for gittin' his eyes ampitated ! "

Jacey clawed the spongy meadow sod with his toes, and looked as if he enjoyed himself. Rome wept copiously. Rheem's voice trembled, but he sturdily pursued his investigation.

" Allie ain't gone, I know, 'cause she's in school."

" Well, she is, too. They got somebody to take her place. And she took Arty."

" Loo wouldn't go ! "

" I bet she would ! They all three had some new clothes on they've been sewin' at all the week."

" Ben said he'd get a house and then send for us," gasped Remus.

" He's been gone to Chicago for three or four days, and he sent down word to the rest when to come, too."

" And they left us ! " wept Maude.

" There isn't a word of it so ! " affirmed Rheem, fiercely.

" Well, you just go over to New Town and see ! " challenged Jacey.

" I will," said Rheem.

" Well, come along," said Jacey.

Maude, clinching with despairing hands the tops
of the pickets, watched her twin striding with manly
steps across the meadow, trailing John White's linen
coat in grandfatherly contrast to Jacey's bare, trot-
ting legs. And I cannot begin to tell you how forsaken and terrified she felt on the big earth, though
it was so bright. Of course; it wasn't all so — a bit!
But, if such a thing could be so! She turned over
the terrible possibilities in her mind, and they rolled
up mountain high. If somebody could take their
lots, and their house could burn down — but no, indeed, the rest of the Bunch would never go off and
leave two of the young ones so!

The sun grew hot before Rheem came back. The
earth steamed, the leaves began to cast startling
shade in the vivid light; but she sat on the pickets,
bare-headed and almost breathless, waiting for her
twin. He appeared at the farther side of the pasture; he came nearer, and, as he approached, Maude
could hear an irrepressible, minor note which
sounded like "boo-hoo!" till he came so near she
could see the tears dripping down his downy rounded
face. The linen coat swayed behind him, and his
little shirt collar was thrown back, as if he could not
bear its pressure on his throbbing neck. Maude
now took flight from her long poise, and flopped over

the fence to stagger up to him, and slide her arm around John White's coat.

"What's the matter, Rheemie? Did that Jacey Dixon hurt you? He's just as naughty as he can be!"

"No," sobbed Remus, now completely broken down, "they *are* gone!"

"Not Ben and Allie?"

"Yes, sir!"

"And Jack and Arty?"

"Yes, they are!"

"And Loo?"

"They've all gone and left us here!"

Oh, desolation! They lifted up their voices and wept together, until Priscilla in the kitchen heard them, and looked out toward the milking pasture to see if anything was the matter with her pet calves. Rome and Remus, behind the farthest palings of the garden, were in another direction.

"Who told you?" asked Maude, clinging to the last straw of hope.

"I went and peeked in at the doctor's, and none of them were there. And I peeked in at the school, and none of them were there. And I saw Mr. Thomas, and he said they *did* go in the early train this morning."

" O, I wish we'd run over last night, then they'd ta⌐en us along ! "

" Humph, I don't ! " said Remus, hotly. " I don't want to stick in where I ain't wanted ! "

" Not wanted ! " repeated Rome, aghast. It was a new view of herself to see herself not wanted in the home Bunch.

" They've gone off and left us," hiccoughed Remus, indignantly. " We can go off by *our*selves, too ! We ain't going to care ! "

Maude was not quite sure for herself.

" I want to see Arty ! " she broke out.

And, upon second thought :

" I want to see Allie and Ben ! "

And, her heart being now wide open :

" I want to see poor Jack — and Loo ! Oh-hoo ! "

" I don't want to see any of 'em ! " said Rheem, with bunched up eyebrows. " I don't care anything about 'em ! "

" Yes, you do ! " said Rome, decidedly. " And, maybe they sent for us and the word didn't get here."

" Ho ! Couldn't get a mile ! "

" Or, maybe they're waiting to buy some new clothes to send back to us."

Remus shook his head, sidewise, this motion in- dicating that clothes were not going to salve his deep indignation at this late day.

"What we going to do?" then inquired his twin.

This dried his eyes and roused his energies.

"We've just got to look out for ourselves!"

Maude believed him, and waited to see which way he would look. But, with feminine tact, she put in a pebble to turn the stream.

"I believe Mrs. White wishes we were at some- body else's house."

" Well, we won't stay much longer at *her* house!"

"Nobody wants us, Rheemie."

"Well, we don't care. Le's sit down and study up what to do."

"We da'sn't here. We'll get Mr. and Mrs. White's clothes dirty. Oh, *Rheem*, why didn't you hold up that coat-tail?"

"I don't care *how* splashed it gets," replied the boy with calm deliberation. "I'll sit down in that puddle with it if I'm a mind to!"

"Don't!" begged his companion in tribulation. " Le's climb over in the woods and find a clean log where it's shady."

This they did. It appeared on reviewing the situa- tion that they were both too dejected to plan with

NOBILITY IN DISGUISE.

any brilliancy ; and moreover, their costumes limited them to very narrow boundaries. They were too honest to carry away the borrowed clothing, which at present served them as a covering, though it did not by any means render them objects of envious admiration. But they were one in wishing to get away from under Priscilla's feet. Their situation as they looked at it was truly desperate. They had a pair of boots, a pair of shoes, some underclothing and a bed-spread between them. No other clothing or portable property. And whither should they depart, since nobody wanted them ? It was a hard problem.

" *We* might go to Chicago, too," suggested Maude, with a sneaking desire to be near the others of the Bunch, in spite of their strange desertion.

"Wouldn't they all stare to see us come walking into town !" speculated Remus, which observation was a very just one when their travelling suits are taken into consideration.

They consulted, and wagged their heads for about sixty minutes by Seth Thomas' slow calculation ; though *he* could know nothing about it, away off in the shaded sitting-room, staring straight ahead of him, and choking regularly every hour.

Priscilla got dinner ready, and thought a great deal about pickling. Her husband rode into the yard before the household sat down, and as soon as he entered the house he asked for the children.

"They're around somewhere," said Priscilla.

"I've brought some clothes for them," said John, opening the sitting-room door and tossing a bundle, directly in front of Seth Thomas' unwinking countenance, to the settee, "and some news," added John. "What move do you think that little tribe has taken now? Doc. Darling says Jack's is a bad case. The eyes are pretty badly hurt; he's afraid the boy'll never see again. Anyhow, he thought the boy better go to a good oculist. It's an expensive thing, and they all broken up and burnt out so. Ben went up to see how he could manage. Those young ones are either lucky or so plucky they won't be beat. He found something to do, and went straight and answered an advertisement in a daily about some rooms, and rented some, and the woman he rented them of took a fancy to him. I suppose the young one told her about his sisters, and she wanted to know if one of them could tend to her housekeeping for her. So Ben, he sends down for the whole pack. And they all pack up except our two. Allie had to buy some ready-made clothes to fit them out, and McKay's to take 'em up to-morrow — he's going up anyhow on business. I reckon they'll pass two such little chaps

over the railroad for nothing, and if they won't, I'll
see they get their fare paid. Allie sent a note telling
them all about it with the clothes. The train stopped
at Carver City for breakfast, and she run up town
and got the things and sent them right back ; Joyce
give 'em to me to bring out. She said she was
uneasy about the two young ones for fear they would
feel cut up at being left a day behind, but it's in
Jack's favor ; they want to get something done for
him as quick as they can. Ho, Rheem !" cried John,
stepping to the edge of the porch, "ho, Maddie!
Come here ! got something for ye. Where *are* they ?"

"Oh, not far off," said Priscilla, "they'll get hungry and come in pretty soon — sit down to dinner."

But Rome and Remus were some distance off,
stepping along in the densest part of the woods, like
a pair of white Siamese twins, the spread folded
equally over their tropical garments, and Rome, feeling more humiliation than her mate who had less
delicacy and more love for adventure, of course, was
saying under her breath with a sob, "It's just as
mean as dirt, so it is ! "

John White, going into the sitting-room to unfold
his weekly paper after dinner, found on the door-step
his linen coat and loaned trousers lying folded nicely
beside Priscilla's long calico basque and overskirt,

and his kind lips pulled themselves away out in front of his face for a mighty whistle. He took one step into the dining-room:

"Jerusalem artichokes, Priscilla!"

CHAPTER XVII.

MISS GAFF AND SMALLER FRY.

CHICAGO opened her arms not unkindly to the Bunch. H o w huge and love-ly she looked to their village eyes ! T h e y came—not by hack, I assure you, n o r b y street car, but quietly patting along on their own feet, through street after street, over crossing after crossing, to the building in which Ben had rented rooms, and Allie, who gave up her school to stay by the others, hoped to find employment. They led Jack between two of them. Arty was a good traveller, and only asked to hold some one's dress or hand while his great eyes took in all the strange sights, and his boots kept time with the family march.

They had no luggage to move.

The house, when they arrived before it, towered high above their heads and was squeezed in a long row of houses, all so exactly alike that they looked like palings in a fence; all painted alike, but with different numbers on their foreheads. It was built of brick and approached by a flight of steps. They approached it and rang the bell. The street was not a stylish one, but it looked very nice, and Loo thought she got a glimpse of the lake from the top of the steps.

" What lake ? " asked Arty, who had been quiet during the whole day's run on the train, absorbing everything with his eyes.

" Lake Michigan," replied Ben.

" What is Lake Michigan ? "

" A great big pond," replied Jack.

The door was opened by a German girl, with a good-natured but stupid look. They made quite a formidable little party on the steps, and she stared at them.

" We are the folks who are to live on the top floor," said Ben.

At this she opened the door wide, and they all entered.

" Is Miss Gaff in ? " inquired Ben.

" No," replied Minnie, in the high key peculiar to German voices. " She gone to see her patients. She been home to dinner-time."

" We'll just go up-stairs," said Ben ; and they proceeded to mount, the girls walking on either side of Jack, and Ben leading Arty, who toiled up flight after flight, puffing louder on every landing.

" My gracious, Ben ! are we going to the sky ? " asked Allie.

" Sometime, I hope. But just now we're going to the fourth floor."

The stairs were uncarpeted, but they were built of dark, rich-colored wood. There was a heavy, substantial air about the whole building.

When they got to the top they found a kind of vestibule, which opened into a set of rooms, five in number. Allie looked around, wondering blankly how she should ever furnish them. They were pretty as they were, however. The walls were finished in rough plaster, and every room done in a particular kind of wood. That one overlooking the street was finished in oak, the one next it in cherry ; a small entry and the bath-room, which divided these two from the rest of the set, were in walnut, and the remainder, being in the darker part of the house, in ash. Real woods, polished, without any varnish. The windows were double, and each sash contained but one pane of plate glass. There were two gas chandeliers, the gas coming through burners at the sides of the rooms. Loo was impressed with the possible beauty of the place, and especially with the grates; there being one in every room except that one designed for the kitchen, where a small range waited.

"We sha'n't have to buy any stoves!" she exclaimed in ecstasy. "These are lots prettier than the old Franklin, too!"

"Isn't the rent awful high?" asked Allie, suspiciously.

"It's two hundred a year," said Ben, "but we might have had to pay half as much more for the worst kind of places. Rents are always high in towns; and mind, Allie, the rent's to come out of what Miss Gaff pays you for keeping house for her."

"I *hope* I'll suit her."

"The reason that we get these rooms so low is, that Miss Gaff bought this house in the row, and she won't take anybody for tenants except folks who happen to please her. She's very particular. I guess our being from the country was a good deal in our favor. There are three floors besides the basement. She has the first floor; the second one's empty, and we took the third. All the families in the house can have their washing done in the basement. There are drying places and all."

"But think," cried housekeeper Loo, "of dragging the water for cooking clear up all those stairs, and carrying slops down —"

"Look here," said Ben, stepping up to the kitchen-sink near which he happened to be. He turned on the cold water, then the steaming hot water, and they all saw it sink away with great admiration. They were initiated into all the mysteries and conveniences of the flat—even Jack, who poked his finger under the hot stream and jumped, saying, "Christopher Columbus!" and, while his quick hands felt silver faucets, or smooth wood, or promising grate, could not help crying out: "Oh, children, I wish I could see!"

"Bless your dear old head!" said Allie, patting his bandages, "you *shall* see after 'while!"

"Jacky," cried Arty, pulling him by the trousers' leg to something he admired, "can't you see this? Jacky, look right tight at it — can't you see it?"

"I'd rather see you, Muggins. Give me a good

square hug, will you? A good square one, mind, not one of your little squeezes."

Jack dropped on his knee, and he and Arty clasped arms around each other for the "squarest" and heartiest kind of an embrace; then Arty put some sugar kisses on the tip of Jack's visible nose, and not a disappointing "dog-kiss," among them. Arty was five years old, but always Jack's baby.

"Now," said Ben, "let's sit down and see how we stand."

This rather contradictory thing they proceeded to do. They camped in a huddle on the polished floor.

"I've got," said the young *pater-familias*, turning out the contents of his pocket-book, "after paying for four of us — Arty was passed — ten dollars! We don't owe a cent in New Town."

"That's a blessing," said Allie, "and," turning out her own portemonnaie, "after paying fifteen dollars for things for Maude and Rheem, and part for the clothes we have on — we girls — I have twenty dollars out of my last month's salary."

"And there was the Association Fund," said Jack, "that we put in Mr. Joyce's safe over at the station."

"We put that into the house, you know."

"O yes, so we did. I'd just drawn *my* money before the house burnt, so I've no cash to stock in, now. I'd 'a got a place to be telegraph-operator, soon," mourned Jack, aside.

"Thirty-five dollars. That's a pretty slim stock to go to housekeeping on!"

"Yes, but it's considerably better than nothing."

"So it is!" they all exclaimed.

"We must pay half a month's rent in advance out of it," said Ben; "but I go right to work the first of the week, and we can get things as we need them. First thing I do, I'll order a load of coal to cook with."

"And where'll we put it?" cried Loo, aghast.

This led to a pilgrimage to the coal-closet, which they found on opening a smooth-finished door in the vestibule.

"The man that brings it will find the closet," said Ben.

Then they camped again. Allie took out her lead-pencil and a bit of paper to make a list of things they needed at once. She hesitated, looked anxious.

"Our rent out, Ben, how much will that leave?"

"Twenty-seven dollars and sixty-two and a half cents."

"Then there will be Rome and Rheem's fare?"

"I think they'll come half price. I'll settle that with Mr. McKay."

"We're under obligations to all the good New Town folks who took us after the fire. I'll crochet white woolen sacques for all Mrs. Darling's babies before Christmas"—then the magnitude of this undertaking appearing to her, Allie, amended, "or, for as many as I can. Well, say we have twenty-seven dollars."

"We'll not need cupboards," said Loo, pointing to the shelved closets.

"And we can camp with very, very few dishes until we get more money. Six plates, six cups, and saucers—O, the spoons, the knives, the forks! how they'll cost!"

"Don't forget assorted platters," put in Loo, "and four or five vegetable covers, and *twelve* little fruits—"

"Loo Dogberry, do you know we shall have to buy every potato and every scrap of fruit we eat? We have no garden, now!"

"We'll *have* to get pots and pans and a broiler—"

"No we shan't," cried Ben, opening a closet beside the end of the range and showing the range's full outfit.

"O, what a blessed place!" cried Loo, in ecstasy.

"What are we going to sleep on?" inquired Jack, whose head was, even then, aching uncomplainingly for a place to lay itself.

The rest stared at each other, aghast.

"If we buy as much as one bed-room set," said Allie, in despair, "it'll take all we've got, and leave nothing to buy food; and we mustn't think of carpets!"

"Why should we?" cried Ben. "They aren't the thing in this kind of a house. Look at the floors! Do you suppose they finished them up in that way to be covered? Miss Gaff says all they ought to have is a drugget in the middle; and we'll buy druggets when we get farther along."

Loo looked at the narrow, glistening boards not unkindly.

"They'll be easily washed," she said.

"I'll go," said Ben, after profound thought, "and buy two large mattresses and a little one, and some coal, and something to eat, and a mighty few dishes. That seems best, doesn't it, Allie? The mattresses will cost about fifteen dollars. We can put 'em up on bedsteads when we can afford the bedsteads. It's so warm we sha'n't need covers."

"That'll do firstrate," said Allie, "and we'll pick our bed-rooms. O, we'll get fixed up lovely one of these days!"

"I tell you, now," cried Jack, "take that hundred dollars of mine and get what you want. You can get it of Mr. McKay, treasurer."

"No, sir," said Ben, firmly, "we won't, my son.

You'll need it all ; and, as to the children's money, we'll never touch that. Suppose anything should happen to us older ones, they'd have nothing to fall back upon."

"Now, Loo," said Allie, " let's make a list of *only* what we must have. Plates, cups — I wonder if we can't do without cups ? — knives — knives and forks. Oh dear !"

" Something to eat, first," begged Ben. "The easiest way would be for us all to go to a restaurant, but we can't afford to think of it. Loo, couldn't you heat the kettle and make some coffee ? And I'll get a baker's big loaf and some potatoes — and I think a beefsteak would be best for us."

They were agreed on that, Loo admonishing her market-bound brother not to forget salt and butter.

" For this time," said she, with alacrity, " when I've broiled the steak, I'll cut it up and put it between slices of bread — with this big knife ; and here's a dipper, we can take turns drinking out of that ! — O, milk, Ben, milk and sugar !"

Ben made memoranda and shook his head.

" We'll have to be *very* careful," said he.

" Ben, what sort of woman is Miss Gaff ? " inquired the bandaged boy, who was obliged to paint inward pictures for himself now.

"Well, she's real nice. She isn't very tall nor very short, but pretty thin."

"Is she pretty?" asked Allie.

"She's — good-looking."

"What did the girl mean by saying she had gone to see her patients?" asked Loo.

"Why, she's a doctor!"

"A doctor! I think a woman doctor must be horrid!"

Jack tugged at his bandages. "Bring her up! Let me see her. I never saw a woman doctor in my life." "I tell you, now, she's smart!" cried Ben. "Anybody could tell that by looking at her, and to see her get into her buggy when it's brought to the door, and pick up the lines and drive off."

"Does she wear a plug hat and carry pill-bags?" asked Jack, excitedly.

"No! what are you talking about! She wears a pretty little hat, and takes her medicine in a kind of case, though I guess she always has a lot more hid about the buggy. She makes lots of money."

"How do you know?"

"When I was here the day I came for rooms, four or five persons called for her. She has her office on the first floor at one side of the hall."

Allie was looking dejected. She did not enjoy the situation.

" I'll have to send coal first, " said Ben, returning to the original subject, as a matter of course, "and I'll send it from the very first coal-yard I see; and some kindling. "

He was going out into the vestibule when a pat of steps coming up the stairs made him pause.

" Here she comes, I do believe ! "

Pat, pat, pat.   Firm, light and swift.

"Oh, you're there, are you, *pater familias ?* Did you bring your family ? "

" Yes, ma'am," replied Ben, pushing the door wide ; " here they are."

Miss Gaff came in among them ; she wore a black cashmere, trimmed with silk, fitting her closely, but trailing slightly ; a gold watch and black woven guard ; her heavy brown hair was coiled on the top of her head, and straight, unruly bits of it strayed into her neck ; spotless collar and cuffs, a round gold brooch; a pleasant face with a reddish tint, large eyes and broad nose : this was Miss Gaff.

An atmosphere of beneficence tempered with a tendency to harmless prejudices, entered with her The children all rose up from the floor.   She made first for Jack:

" Why, what's the matter with the little man's eyes ? "

" He was the one that got burnt, ma'am. "

' " Badly ? "

"So he's been bandaged ever since. You know I told you that our house burned down?"

"Yes; and I must have a look at those eyes."

She turned towards Allie: "This is your oldest sister?"

"Yes, ma'am, the one that is to keep house for you. And this is Loo and this is our baby, Arty."

Miss Gaff shook hands with all of them; she had a long, slender white hand, soft, but firm to the touch.

"Well, make yourselves at home," said she. "Of course, Miss Allie, you'll want to get things running comfortably up here before you begin with me. How do you like the flat?"

The Bunch chorused heartily that they thought it was splendid.

Miss Gaff led them over it again, and showed them conveniences which they had not discovered.

"When will your furniture come?" she asked.

The Bunch looked at each other, and from smiling shamefacedly, proceeded on to a broad laugh.

"When we earn it, ma'am!" said Ben.

"Oh, you lost everything in the fire. That was too bad."

"Yes, ma'am, and we're obliged to go slow in getting things till we can make things work around right again."

" It was too bad, " repeated Miss Gaff.   " But I thought there were seven of you ? "

" The twins are coming on to-morrow. "

" Twins, eh ?   Well, how are you going to arrange your rooms ?"

It was very easy to be confidential with Miss Gaff. They all ran and showed her which room was to be the boys', which the girls', which the dining-room and which the parlor.   She was very cheerful and business-like.   And for their encouragement told them how hard she had worked in her own life, first to support herself after her father, who had been worth several hundred thousand dollars, failed ; and next to learn her profession and next to get established in it.

" But there are people now, " said Miss Gaff, enthusiastically, to the Bunch, with pardonable pride in her success, " who have faith in no other physician, and who telegraph back to me for orders when they leave the city.   Some of the very ones who thought medicine was not a fit calling for a woman ! "

She was full of oddities, and queer confidences and kind impulses.   She was a lady about thirty-six years old, with an older benignity about her which suited her style and profession.

Ben offered her half a month's rent in advance.

This was simply a guaranty of good faith on his part, for the arrangement was that she should pay Allie a hundred a year over and above the rent—if the plan proved mutually agreeable. But coming in without bag or baggage, Ben and Allie both felt that their respectability demanded an advance, for fear unforeseen circumstances might terminate the engagement before it was fairly entered into on Allie's part.

Miss Gaff put their money back into Ben's pocket-book herself, strapped it up and told him not to let her hear of it again. She then told them all to come down and dine with her, and would hear of no excuses, after which she went down-stairs and Ben took Allie with him to select such necessary articles as their money would buy. They ordered coal and bought matresses ; and having fully thirty-five dollars since the rent was not deducted, gratefully got a table and some towels, besides the kitchen supplies, Ben at first proposed. The table-ware demanding time and consideration, they postponed selecting any until next morning, for Miss Gaff might wait dinner for them.

" We'll picnic for breakfast, " said Allie.

Minnie did not let them in. She was serving up dinner. Miss Gaff's coachman opened the door and showed them into a parlor through the second door in the hall. It was a very queer parlor. The other

children had been rung down and were surrounding
Miss Gaff, while she showed them some of the bottle
wonders of her museum. One whole end of the
room was a cabinet, carefully covered with glazed
doors to keep dust and meddlesome fingers out of
Miss Gaff's treasures. She had pickled toads and
snakes of the strangest species, from the flat-headed
copper-snake of the North, to the asp of Egypt. She
had a shark's jaws with three rows of horrible notched
teeth in it; an Aztec's skull; fossil pappooses; res-
urrection plants looking like dried branches, but when
she put one in water it spread out delicately, as full
of life as the freshest flower; minerals and fossils
without number, all labelled and in the nicest order;
a stone full of garnets, and any quantity of quartz
with heavy gold streaks leading through it. Miss
Gaff seemed to have pushed these precious minerals
into a corner, and rather to dislike the sight of them,
at which the children wondered, but they afterwards
learned why. The beloved part of her collection
was the bottled monsters; she pointed at the beauty
of their construction and gave an animated little lec-
ture on their habits in life. Arty, however, was best
pleased with an exhibition she gave them with a little
gray cone, the size of your thumb-end. She touched
a match to the tip—it began to hiss and rise up, scaly

fold over scaly fold till it lay a coil-of-dust-snake on the table. He never saw such a firework before.

Minnie rang the bell and Miss Gaff led her guests out to dinner. Loo was crowded back, and making a misstep pushed the door behind her; something began to clatter in that corner at the end of the cabinet: she looked, and sprang straight up with a shriek, for there was a human skeleton dancing airily on nothing and seeming to make fantastic offers of its hands to give her a swing !

" Oh, don't be startled, " said Miss Gaff, looking back; "its only Bony ; I dissected and put him together myself—with some assistance about cleaning the bones. "

Loo felt profound respect for Miss Gaff, but her flesh crept on her own bones in spite of reasoning.

" Hollo ! what's this ? " exclaimed Ben, " I'm stepping on something."

"Let me see. Why, it's one of my little shell-turtles ! "

" It's a rosette off a slipper, isn't it ? " asked Allie.

But she dropped it like a coal as its pointed tail and groping head appeared and disappeared.

Miss Gaff laughed, and gathering it up tenderly carried it into the dining-room and placed it in a sort of terrapin-pen, where tortoise-backs in as many stages of development as Mrs. Darling's babies were slowly disporting themselves. Before sitting down to table she showed them her aquarium, which was beautiful. Miss Gaff allowed no one to attend to it but herself, and built up the arch of stones in the middle of it a-fresh every morning.

" I always rise at about five o'clock, " she said. " I cannot sleep in the morning, and it usually keeps me till business hours finding my pets and renovating their houses. Where is Stripey ? " she exclaimed, looking about blankly; " why, he's slipped out of his box into the room, some place ! "

" Who is Stripey ? " asked Loo, beginning to feel cold streaks down her spine.

" Oh, he's my little spotted snake—but you needn't feel afraid of him a mite, he's perfectly harmless —"

" O — o — oh ! " cried Allie, with a little shriek — " something's on my foot — round my ankle ! "

And in sympathy with her the children all began to execute a kind of war-dance.

Miss Gaff, laughingly, stooped down and disentangled her pet from the trembling girl, and held him up in her hands, to show how harmless he was. But his scaly back, his sinuous length and diamond points of eyes made them instinctively shudder with ancient hatred of the snake, while they sincerely tried to admire.

"Naughty boy," cooed Miss Gaff, while she put him back into a box half full of earth, and furnished with all the conveniences of snake domestic life, "did he get out and look all over de house for his mistress, and get on de strange lady's ankle? He often coils round my feet," she explained to the Bunch, "and lies sunning himself there while I am studying, with the tip of his tail curled around his neck, as contentedly as a kitten."

The children tried to fancy his snakeship purring, to complete the picture of his innocence. They sat down to table and found a bountiful dinner. There was roast veal, a great variety of vegetables, but first of all a very nice soup; and dessert plates of pie and an iced pudding, with cheese, waited on the side-board for the change.

"Minnie cooks decently," said Miss Gaff, "but she needs some one to look after her all the time. Now she has forgotten to put on the salts!" She touched a bell, Minnie appeared, and breathing apologies when she found what was wanted, produced the salt-bottles from a shelf of the side-board.

As she came in, a bound, a scuffle and a bark followed her, and six dogs, wagging their tails nearly off and all attracted to Miss Gaff as planets are pulled to the sun, jumped up in bunches and by pairs, and singly on the back of her chair, licking her face.

" Why, why, why ! " exclaimed Miss Gaff, who had now finished pouring the coffee, "couldn't dey stay out one evening, but must dey come to see dey mistis anyhow ? "

" Yowp ! " yelled the Newfoundland.

" Woo — wooh ! " declared the snowy Spitz.

" Wee — e ! " whined an ebony-nosed terrier twisting himself nearly in two with delight.

" Bowwh ! " burst out Lucky, a house-dog, so heavy and awkward and large that his tail, which kept up a circular motion like a windmill, was in danger of knocking over something or some small person.

Wix, a shaggy black and white mongrel who looked like a dwarfed Newfoundland, went off into a succession of barks, and a very slender, graceful hound placed his paws on the table and looked at all the company.

" Shall I put them out, ma'am ? " asked Minnie, about to return to the kitchen.

" No; let them be ; they want to get acquainted with the folks. Wix, my little boy, put your hair out of your eyes ! "

Wix, whose shaggy locks half hid his bright orbs, certainly made great efforts with his tail, but wag he never so hard, he couldn't wag his eyes clear. Miss

Gaff gave him a bite of veal and all the other dogs made a focus of their noses in the spot where Wix snapped it. Arty was greatly amused, but he drew his legs up under him when the hound's cold nose investigated the backs of them.

" Do — they — stay in the kitchen ? " inquired Alice, with some hesitation.

Miss Gaff laughed. " Were you ' going to give notice ' if they did ? "

" Oh, no ! " exclaimed Allie.

" They have a kennel of their own in the back yard," continued their mistress ; " a separate apartment for every dog in it. They get along splendidly together. I daren't let them run in the streets, so I give them the run of my rooms. Sometimes I take one or two in the buggy with me. They are quite a happy family. "

The dogs, whose voices had been joining in a low growl over a plate Miss Gaff had filled and set for them, with a napkin under it, on the carpet, now raised a terrific snarl and several yelps, while Wix came toward her carrying one paw, and tears in his eyes if one could see them.

" You naughty boys ! " cried their mistress, " just when I'm telling how peaceable you are ! Did they bite his foot ? "

She reached down and took the plate away from them, and they all wagged their tails and squatted in pleading repentance ; but not another morsel were they allowed to have before company ; she made them all go and sit in a disconsolate row by the wall, where they blinked, or licked their chops or snapped at a fly—excepting Wix, whose foot had fallen a prey to some of his brethren's ill-nature ; him she allowed to sit beside her skirt, and this favor so elated him that he beat the floor with his tail to that degree it seemed he would either break through into the cellar or irreparably damage his tail. As dinner proceeded and Miss Gaff's protecting kindness towards all creatures became more and more apparent, the children were quite fascinated by her. Their company seemed good for her, also ; she was very attentive to their wants, and as busy as the matron of a very large orphan asylum. She ate very little herself, but Allie observed she was an exquisite epicure, and even disturbed by the way dishes were set on the table. Allie resolved when she took Miss Gaff's housekeeping in hand, to take the table-laying into her own hands and make a fine art of it. Minnie changed their plates, and they took dessert. Miss Gaff had new coffee made and ordered down a certain old set of painted china cups to drink the dessert coffee from.

" By the way, " said she, "have you bought table-
ware yet ? "

" We're going out to pick some in the morning, "
began Ben.

"You needn't. I have a dinner set in the closet
that I never use — I don't like the pattern, and I like
to mix my table-ware now, and not have things so
uniform. You can use it till you get rich and proud
enough to refurnish your table according to your
minds. "

" But if anything should get broken, " said Loo,
anticipating the distress of such an accident.

" Pooh ! Take it and use it. Minnie, wash up
that dinner set we never use, and take it up-stairs.
Come here, sirs," said Miss Gaff, immediately, bringing the dogs out to turn aside any grateful speeches,
"now sit up ! "

They all set on their haunches, the Newfoundland,
the lubber, the hound, the Spitz, the terrier and Wix.
Their fore paws hung down helplessly and their tails
moved in meek chorus. She gave a little speech on
the duties of dogs in civilized communities, and dis-
missed them with a pat upon the head of each, and
they went to their kennel to be fed by Minnie. Miss
Gaff took the children back into the parlor, and having noticed that they could examine curiosities with-

out handling or injuring them, she begun a little
business chat with Allie. She liked the girl's fresh,
lady-like appearance. Allie was now twenty, but
looked much younger; the school-room had given
her manners a certain precision, but country freedom
and the constant company of the rest of the Bunch
had kept her face undinted and unfaded.

" I have two people, " said Miss Gaff : " Minnie,
and Jacob, my coachman. His room is in the basement, and he takes care of himself. Minnie does
the laundry-work in another part of the basement.
She is a good girl and, not very wasteful ; but I need
some one to oversee the house all the time. I don't
like her to touch this room except when I am by ;
she has no idea of the value of a collection. Do you
see ? "

" Yes, ma'am," said Allie timidly.

" Well, I have my dresses done out of the house,
always. But I never get a morsel of time for plain
sewing and the house suffers for it. I'll show you my
rooms, " said Miss Gaff ; which she did. Her own
chamber was a sort of gymnasium, with trapezes, Indian clubs, dumb-bells and health-lift. " I take exercise before I dress, in the morning, " she explained,
" after my bath."

There were besides her private rooms, a kitchen

and pantries, the dining-room, a store room and Minnie's bed-chamber. All of these were abundantly
furnished. Allie was to sleep up-stairs with her sister, which pleased her, but the rest of her life was
to be below.

" I don't want you to imagine, " said Miss Gaff,
" that you must stay close here, like a prisoner. Only
keep a supervision of everything — as if it were *your*
house instead of mine. "

Sweet Alice began to feel solid satisfaction in the
prospect. She received keys and a set of account
books, and declared herself ready to begin next day,
for the Bunch's domestic affairs were in a state which
her presence could not help ; and Loo was the trained
housekeeper.

Jack groped for an ottoman and pushed it up in
front of Miss Gaff.

" I wish our other two children were here," said
he, "and I wish I could see you. " His tone was
one of such undisguised admiration that Miss Gaff
laughed.

" I want to examine your eyes, my son, first thing
in the morning. You're going to Dr. Marlowe's ? "

" Yes, ma'am. "

" He's very good — very good in his specialty. I'll
drive you round there when I start on my rounds,
and get his opinion. "

" You're real good," said Jack.

" I wish Maud and Rheem could see these, " Loo was remarking, uncertain whether they should ever again have the *entree* of this museum-parlor. " Miss Gaff, " she called out mildly, " didn't these beautiful yellow-streaked white rocks come out of a gold mine ? "

" Yes, " snapped Miss Gaff, pulling her eyebrows together so that a deep, upright wrinkle stood between them, " that's where father's money went. Mines, mines, mines ! And after losing everything else in speculating he lost himself prospecting a mine."

" How ? " begged the Bunch.

" Disappointment and fever," said Miss Gaff. " Don't speak about it any more. I never talk of it." She reached out and took the hand of Arty who was leaning against his eldest sister, and telling Loo to " never mind " when that tender hearted girl tried to apologize, began to talk nervously to him in German, much to his astonishment.

" *Bübchen, wie befinded sie sich ?* "

" Yes, ma'am," said Arty, widening his eyes.

" *Ach, so ?* " said Miss Gaff, laughing. " *Sprachen sie ein lied :*

> "*Die Rose, die Lily, die Taube, die Sonne,*
> *Sie liebt Ich ernst alle in liebes wonne :*
> *Ich liebt sie nicht mehr, Ich liebe* "———

" I can't *understan'* that," said Arty.

The bell rung. Miss Gaff was in request to see a patient on the other side of the city. She called for Jacob and the phæton immediately, and had her hat and gloves and sacque on, to a nicety, her case ready and her remedies forecast, before the Bunch could marshal themselves to bid her good evening. They went up-stairs and she drove off.

"I'm glad the twins will sleep more comfortably than we do, to-night," said Alice, when the matresses were brought up from a dray, and she gazed at bandaged Jack, and felt how cool the lake winds could be even on summer nights.

Rome and Remus were at that moment stretching their weary limbs under a walnut tree, and looking up at the dark sky.

CHAPTER XVIII.

CHILDREN OF THE WOOD.

IT was a fine spreading walnut tree, in fact a noble specimen of its class, but it didn't seem to suit them.

"If we weren't so tired we'd look for a *holler* tree," said Remus.

"Yes," responded Rome, "I'd rather be in a hollow one. But *bears* get in them, don't they?"

Remus was cross: he was hungry: he was beaten back.

"I just as lieves as not one would eat us up."

Maude demurred. "I don't want to be eat up. I rather have something to eat myself!"

They cuddled quietly awhile. It was a warm evening in the woods; the murderous mosquitoes were thick, and hunted the children till they hid clear under the spread which looked like a collapsed tent. Occasionally an industrious mosquito bored through this and brought the blood and a start out of their unprotected little bodies.

Rome's mind was busy with stories of children lost in the woods, and a " large animal bounding out of the bushes towards them." In the story it always turned out to be the family dog seeking them, but in their case she knew it would prove a bear if not a lion or an elephant ! If a rabbit startled the grass her heart jumped.

"What'll we do for breakfast, Rheemie ? " she inquired, facing between whiles their prospect of indefinite fasting.

Rheem snored.

She repeated her question. He snored louder. From this delicate hint she gathered that the mind masculine did not wish to be disturbed further, and she took a turn in the spread and tried to snug down in the roots of the tree. They had two deep little cribs, tolerably cushioned with leaves, but the ants were there before them and came out and bit the intruders.

" I can't stand this ! " cried Remus forgetting his snore and bouncing out of his crib.

" Neither can I ! " cried Rome, bouncing up also.

" Let's climb the tree and sleep in the limbs," suggested her brother, and she agreed rather doubtfully.

They pulled themselves up the shaggy trunk of the
walnut, and when they reached the first large limbs
Remus had an inspiration : he bade his twin stand and
hold by the trunk till he fixed what he meant to, and
she watched in wonder.   He ripped the spread down
the centre and tied the halves in tremendous knots to
even limbs, making two pretty white hammocks.   He
tested the strength of both hammocks himself and
showed Maude how reliable they were.   She crept
into hers and lay down in ecstecy, slightly lessoned by
the hold which a persevering mosquito had upon her
shoulder.   It was ten feet above the ground, but the
knots were stout ; it was near enough to her twin for
her to reach over and touch his head if she got frightened, and deep enough for her to roll over without
tumbling out.   They swung like a pair of complacent
bats and fought mosquitoes with renewed energy.   All
they needed now was food and clothing and a pocket
map of the road to Chicago to which city by tacit
agreement they were making their way, to overwhelm
with surprise and remorse the seceded part of the
family.

A mother-bird up higher in the tree, stirred and

scolded her wakeful babies. Rome started up and grasped Remus.

"It's a Bugaboo!"

"'Tisn't! It's a bird."

Rome nestled again and slapped mosquitoes. How fierce was their droning war-cry, how sudden and sharp their attacks, how persistent their boring.

"Let's tell stories," said Remus, swinging his hammock and pretending to be in a state of oriental enjoyment.

"I wish I could hear Arty make some," sighed Rome, " he's so cunning! Don't you remember that one he used to say about ' There was an old woman sat down to 'pin, and she heard somefin go boo-ah! boo-ah! boo-ah! and she looked up and there was a great big bugaboo bear.'"

"Oh, pshaw!" snuffed Remus, glancing around the darkened landscape over the side of his hammock, "who wants to hear about bears?"

" Wouldn't you be scared if you'd see one? Bears can climb trees, can't they!"

" There *aren't* any in these woods; they were all killed off long ago."

" Rheemie, did you ever hear the story about the hunter that a bear ate up? When the country was new. I guess it was in these woods. I always got scared when I thought about it. The folks found his boot and his gun and his bed. Oh Rhemie, how'll he resurrect out of the bear and how'll his head resurrect to the rest of him ? "

Maude was quite overcome and shut her eyes, shuddering.

"Keep still," hushed Remus, which caution made his twin grab at him and cry out in a startled voice — " Why ? "

Her own ears told her why. A swish, swish, swish of shrubs and a crackle of dry sticks on the ground announced the near presence of something. She cowered like a little lady snail in her shell.

"Hullo, you, up there! have you hung yourselves ? "

Remus now cowered too, half in dread and half in shame ; it was John White's voice ; the dear old fellow who was always pulling them out of scrapes, stood at the foot of the tree.

"I heard you talking, so you needn't hide! What's that you've swung up — that white stuff? "

"Our spread," piped Maude, looking down at him, her heart lightened by the sight, though they had run away from his house.

"Well, what are you doing here ? Have you turned out to run wild in the woods? "

"We're going to Chicago," said Remus, showing his head.

"Yes, you look like it! 'Rockaby baby on the tree top, when the wind blows the cradle will rock." Well, what's the matter with you youngsters, anyhow? Went off without your dinner, or any clothes — kept me hunting for you all the afternoon ; you ought to have told Priscilla if you wanted to have a scamper in the woods ; we've been uneasy about you."

"She said we were underfoot," burst from Rome's troubled bosom.

"Oh!" laughed John, and he chuckled awhile under the tree ; "she can cook good dinners, though," he added by way of apology for Priscilla.

"The rest went off and left us," said Rheem, shaking his head with some threatening intimation of what he would do yet.

"And Jacey Dixon said they didn't want us,' added Rome ; "and we had no clothes and no money, and we were going to Chicago to show 'em we could come anyhow!"

"We wasn't goin' to tag 'em, though!" corrected Remus with spirit.

"Yes. Well, Jacey Dixon usually tells the whole truth and nothing but the truth, doesn't he? For instance, the time he saw Arty going to the old tannery in Billy's rag-sack ? "

" I went my own self and asked Mr. Thomas, too, and *he* said they'd all gone to Chicago."

" And did he say they had to leave you on account of buying ready-made clothes to send back ? and that Lawyer McKay was to take you up to-morrow ?   He'll be disappointed when he calls for you and finds you're not there," said John.

He smiled.   The hammocks both gave an uneasy squirm.

" Allie got off at Carver City, and ran up street while the train waited for breakfast, and bought clothes to send right back to you ; she sent a note, too. Mr. Joyce gave me the bundle at noon ! " John added, more as a soliloquy than a remark, " Priscilla might have made them some things, but she's so busy with house-work I guess she didn't think about it."

Rome and Remus leaned over the sides of their hammocks with sheep-faced looks which the dusk could not veil.

" Hadn't you better come down," said John, " and go home and have some supper ?   I guess you can stand our house one night more ! "

His thrust and the rankling of family troubles quite pierced Maude's tender heart.   She began to cry.

Remus crawled out of his hammock and began to untie it, with sturdy grunts at every hard pull.

"I like to stay at your house first-rate, Mr. White—(uh!)—but I thought we oughtn't stay there always—(uh!)—and we didn't know what they meant. Ben said he'd send word what we were to do—(uh!)—this is hard to untie!"

"He did send word from Chicago: Jack's eyes were so bad they started with him almost as soon as they got the word. He has to be doctored."

"Jacey Dixon said he was blind as a fish-worm!" wept Maude, adding this to her general grief.

"Well, so he may be," said John, gravely, "if something isn't done for him early." He reached up his arms to take the wandering little girl down as she scrambled backwards. Remus unfastened the other hammock and dropped with both of them. He and Rome wrapped themselves up like Choctaws. Remus hung back but Maude was glad to return to civilized life. John White gave one of his forefingers to each of them, and these new Children of the Wood, trotted along beside him as trustfully as the less fortunate ones of the old story went with their bad uncle.

He said nothing more to upbraid them, but all that great mountain of remorse which they were going to pile on their family, rolled back upon themselves!

Said Remus to Mr. White — incidentally:

"I hope the rest won't hear about — our thinking they'd left us. It might hurt their feelings!"

" I hope they won't," said John.

" Do you suppose Mr. McKay will tell them?"

" Not unless somebody tells him."

" Doesn't everybody at your house know we came off?"

"I guess nobody knows the whole thing but Priscilla and I, and Priscilla never talks much; that's a good thing," said John, slily, "quietness is."

" Yes, it is," said Remus.

"Now I'll tell you what to do. You can slip in the front way; the bundle of things is on the settee. You can pick them out and put them on before you come to supper. They're waitin' supper for me, and the rest'll all be on the back porch, or about. And we needn't say that you took off my coat and pants and Priscilla's things, for fear of s'iling them before you started on your ramble!"

Rome rubbed her cheek against the big forefinger which led her and said, " You're the loveliest man I ever saw in the world!"

CHAPTER XIX.

JIPPETY.

The rest of the Bunch did not hear of the twins' distrust and flight, therefore, until they burst into Miss Gaff's top flat and told it themselves! going from one member of the family to another with kisses and penitent squeezes. Mr. McKay brought them to the street door and left them : he was too busy to climb up and see his wards that day, and they were glad of it when they considered the unfurnished state of their rooms. He told Allie the two young children came over the road for nothing, when she offered their fare to him ; and assuring her he would look in on the Bunch the next time he came up, he hurried off.

Like bees in a bee-hive, the Bunch fell to system-

atic work. Ben was employed in building: but
before he had been in the city many weeks his ambi-
tion took definite shape. He meant to learn architecture ; the architect under whom he was working
proved a friend to him, and though all he could then
earn was scant for the family emergencies, he looked
forward to a career of satisfaction and success. All
his spare time he put upon his favorite study ; he had
the free use of the architect's office, evenings, and
it never saw a more earnest thinker and planner than
Ben. He got himself opportunities to see the best
buildings in the city; he was always going about with
pencil and paper in his hands or just inside his vest
pocket. Loo did her best with the home ; her work
was lightened, too, by so many conveniences. By de-
grees the necessary furniture came in, then a rug or
two. Miss Gaff forced bed-clothing upon them until
they could buy some ; the boy's room was made cosy ;
then the girls added comforts to their own ; so by
stages they got another comfortable footing in life.

The first time Remus went to look at the city he
felt as if he had come into a fortune. A new indus-
try rose up before him. Of course he and Maude
were sent to one of the ward schools, but there were
the mornings and evenings — and the morning and
evening papers ! He set up as a newsboy; his pink

cheeks and bright eyes and crisp business manner gained him customers; there were business men whom he regularly waylaid and who regularly bought his paper. Maude felt a thrill of pride when she heard his voice ring out in the street : "Inter-Ocean, sir? — Journal? have a paper? Here's your Inter-Ocean," &c. The little fellow paid a regular weekly sum into the family fund, and kept some nice ten-cent pieces over. It was well he could help, for Allie could only give them the rent now, a help they did not feel, never having paid rent in their lives, and Jack was in darkness.

Poor Jack was driven by Miss Gaff according to her promise, to the oculist's the very next day after his arrival. The doctor did not say very much, but shook his head at Miss Gaff. Jack was jolly, but it did not suit his temperament to sit and be waited on, or to be led "like an old blind beggar" by one of the Bunch to the oculist's for treatment.

"Get me a little dog and string," said Jack, "and a tin cup for the pennies. 'Pity a poor blind man, good people! This helpless being with a family of six children dependent upon him, was blown up in a powdermill and came down without eyesight!'"

After some days he was made to lie still all day long in a darkened room, and dieted sparely. Then

Arty played around him and probably kept him from despairing. Maude came in and told him the wonderful things which happened at school; Remus pictured the glories of journalism (*i. e.*, the selling of the journals); Ben talked architecture to him; Loo told him when the lake looked particularly blue in the glimpse she had of it over the housetops : Allie came up-stairs, put her arm under his dear, old aching head and gave him his dinner with a spoon. And Miss Gaff was a whole host of entertainers; Jack rejoiced when he heard her coming, snapping guitar strings in her throat—an inimitable habit she learned when a child. She thought of a hundred ways to divert him.

"If I turn out blind," said he, " I don't know of anything I can do except grind an organ, with Arty for a monkey. Will you go and be monkey for Jacky, my man ? "

Oh, yes, Arty would be monkey.

"I can telegraph," said Jack; " I can read dispatches by ear easy enough, and work the machine with my eyes shut. I wish I had a battery here."

Miss Gaff brought up to him not a battery, but a small patent machine on which he could tap messages and keep in practice. This pleased him so much that she meditated on putting a real battery within his reach, for at that time she had her own opinions about Jack's ever being able to see again.

She gathered the Bunch on the first Sunday of their settlement under her wing — or rather over her head, and carried them to her church and Sabbath-school. There might be other places of worship in the city of Chicago, but Miss Gaff would have none of them. By her gardening hand the Dogberry Bunch were carefully planted in that church and watered with Bible lessons every Sunday. She was very learned in Bible lore and a person of great influence in the church, and they were very glad to get into such a Sabbath family party, instead of venturing, shy, unstylish and lonely, into the great rich churches to worship.

As soon as Alice had time to collect her thoughts and sit down for a comfortable half-hour undisturbed, she wrote to Joslyn at Hot Springs, telling him all that had befallen her house, and the changes in their base and prospects. But she added, she had great hopes of Jack's eyes, and Ben was happier than ever before in the chances before him, and Loo thought gas, and hot and cold water in the house were *so* nice, and Rheem, the dear little fellow, had taken, of his own accord, to selling papers, and both he and Maude were improving faster in those graded schools than she ever imagined possible, while Arty was growing

so nicely, and was full of wonder and interest in everything. As for herself, she never knew how tired she
was of the school-room until she left it to be Miss
Gaff's housekeeper. And Miss Gaff was so nice ! It
was a wonder how many nice people there were in
the world ! She sent her dearest love to Miss Wylie,
and hoped she might inprove in health every day:
she repeated her *very dearest* love — for that little old
lady of a past generation had a tender hold on Allie.
She closed with kind messages to his mother, and
gave him their present address, telling him if he came
to Chicago the Bunch would be heart-broken if he
passed them over.

Allie's business at Miss Gaff's was exactly suited to
her tastes. She had a pretty bijou home to control.
" Bony " was not a pleasant companion, but she grew
to have a kind feeling towards even him ; the snake
and the turtles and dogs grew endurable, and she
was allowed to lessen their territory ; they kept to
themselves in a sort of Arctic torpor, until Miss Gaff's
evening return, like the return of the sun, thawed them
out to frisky demonstration. Miss Gaff had a library
of finely selected books, and quite a little gallery of
costly and exquisite pictures. She kept this as sacred
as Bluebeard's room until her confidence in and affection for Allie opened all the doors to that young housekeeper.

Allie superintended the table, and took care of the clothes when they came from the laundry, and kept the rooms pretty, as only a tasteful, refined girl can do, and after some instruction and experience, did the marketing, with a very great relish for it. She delighted to go out very early and tread her way among all the odd assemblage on market mornings, to consider Miss Gaff's taste in this or that, and to plan the bill of fare so as to secure the greatest variety at the least cost. It pleased her greatly to see Miss Gaff lift her eyebrows over some unexpected luxury at table, and to hear her exclaim, " Bless us, my child! what a treasure ! " Miss Gaff sat at the head of the table, and Allie sat opposite, the lady doctor declaring they made quite a comfortable family. She received a certain sum every week for current expenses, and kept accounts strictly. On Saturday evening she made a full report to Miss Gaff and closed the account for the week. It was very satisfactory to Allie.

As the greater part of her salary went to cancel the rent, to be sure she had little for her personal expenses. I have yet to see the young lady who will admit that one hundred dollars a year — twenty-five dollars a quarter — is adequate pin-money ! Allie applied her first twenty-five dollars principally to family purposes. But then Allie was one of those girls who have a talent for looking pretty with very small outlay.

Summer went by and the Industrial Exposition opened with the Autumn. Mr. McKay wrote Ben that the Dalrymple trustee had put up an elevator on their old garden spot, and New Town was now a grain market for the surrounding farm lands. He said he had examined into the titles very carefully, and there was no doubt the Dogberry title was defective, and nothing but a quit-claim from the original owners would ever straighten matters, and from possession being already taken it did not seem probable the Dalrymple estate would be inclined to compromise matters. He was very sorry; though on the other hand, he was glad the children were doing so well.

CHAPTER XX.

JIPPETY. — (*Continued.*)

ONE day Alice received a letter from Joslyn containing the news of Mrs. Wylie's death. She had reached home before she died, but only lingered a few days after they brought her back to Danport. She went to sleep holding Joslyn's hand between her two soft shrivelled palms, and did not wake again.

Allie was arranging her dinner-table when the postman rung with this letter. Miss Gaff took luncheon at eleven past, and dined between four and five, unless she had guests to delay dinner. So it happened that the doctor found her housekeeper shedding some tears over this letter as she came in fresh from a brisk drive. She put her kind arm around Allie's broad shoulders. She spoke cheerily, with one of her bright smiles.

"Why, what's the matter, my dear! And I bringing you such good news!"

"Mrs. Wylie is dead. She was a lovely old lady, and so kind to me. She was very old."

"She developed fully, she lived her life as a woman, and passed into ripe old age, did she? Well, don't cry, my child. We mourn for those who die violent deaths or whose disregard of the laws of life cuts them off. Idiots!" cried Miss Gaff, mounting one of her hobbies and beginning to gallop. "When I see every day what fools people are, and how they misuse themselves and entail misery on their children and then lay the blame on Providence, it makes me so mad I can hardly stand it! Where did this Mrs. Wylie live?" she added mildly, climbing down from her hobby.

"In Danport. Cousin Joslyn says he and his mother have devoted nearly their whole time and thoughts to her this summer."

"She is gone like a ripe sheaf of wheat. When you and I die I hope we shall be full of deeds if not of days. You may ring in dinner now."

"Oh, my good news," added Miss Gaff as they sat down. " I have the latest news about Jack."

" The doctor thinks his eyes will get well ! " cried Allie.

" Yes, but he's not to know too soon, or he'll tear the bandages off and be wanting to rush out at his precious railroad work. I'm glad to see you brighten up."

This news Allie found time to communicate to Loo immediately after dinner and Loo and she squeezed each other ecstatically but very quietly, for Jack's ear was by this time nicely educated. Then Loo whispered it to Ben when he came home, and she and Ben shook hands upon it for several seconds. Arty and the twins were not there. It being Saturday afternoon they were at the people's cheap show, the Exposition.

It was the second week of the Exposition, and Remus, to whom it had an inexpressible charm, had " done " it once or twice before. The first time he took Loo, grandly paying her way out of his newsboy money ; and now he felt quite competent to conduct his twin and the baby through the crowds. He set his red lips firmly and told Arty not to be afraid, that great noise was only machinery set in motion. Nothing was more fascinating to Arty, though he felt safer if he held by Rheem's pocket. Some grown-up people jostled them, and one mountainous Dutch woman almost swept them down like sail boats, as she, a full rigged Great Eastern, rushed past.

"Here, take my arm," said Remus to his mate, "and Arty, you better let me lead you. We can keep together nicer." So with Rome on his arm and the baby by the hand, like some complacent *pater-familias* he proceeded to show them the Exhibition. They passed rows of buzzing saws and belted wheels, whole acres, it appeared to Maude, of roaring machinery, a balmy hot-house air lulling their senses, and the immense sky-lighted roof seeming to wander and roll out new panoramas above them. The country children had never seen anything so delightful. They came to a grotto and a fountain, and Rome could hardly believe her eyes; there were flowers on every hand, and beautiful merchandise displayed in the most enchanting manner. There was a bed-chamber elegantly furnished, with even a grate and mantel in it, and hung in satin, lace pillow-cases, lace counter-pane — prettier than the friend's room which was just finished when their house burned down.

"But I tell you now," cried Rheem, drawing his charges away from the displays of wax dolls and toy carriages and every other desirable plaything, "before we look at these things or go up into the gallery

I want you to see the pictures! My goodness, Rome you never saw such a lot, and they're nicer than mother's drawings were, too."

"O Rheem," cried Rome incredulously. But when they promenaded the picture rooms she was constrained to own it.

A different sort of people appeared to frequent the picture room, quite different from the rushers and jostlers and searchers they met in the great hall. There were a great many people sitting here with catalogues in their hands and glasses to their eyes, silently enjoying or criticising paintings.

The children wandered through room after room, Remus reserving his grand sight till the last.

" Now, come on," said he, " I'll see what the man 'll let us in for," and he turned down a quiet passage, lined with printed admonitions to "go and see the chariot race."

"How much will you let us in for, Mister?" said he.

"Three?—three little fellows? The admission is twenty-five cents a person."

"But we're such little fellows."

"Oh, Rheemie," cried his twin in a shrill whisper, "where you going! and spending money to see a race! Arty might get run over and killed."

"I guess you may all go in for thirty cents," said the man. So Remus paid down three dimes with manly precision, and they rounded a canvas screen and entered a gas-lighted room, where perhaps twenty people were at that time sitting on rows of chairs or standing in groups, contemplating Wagner's grand Chariot Race. Rome caught her breath : child as she was the intense life of the picture thrilled her through and through. A row of gas-jets brought it into startling relief. The three little Berries stood looking up at it with pure joy. How quaint they were themselves in their unstylish clothes and clear country coloring !

"We'll get a seat," whispered Remus reverently, drawing his family as he tip-toed forward.

A very beautiful girl, letting her opera-glass sink in her bare tinted hand, watched the group ; her lips curved at the corners, her teeth just glanced between them. She called the attention of a middle-aged lady at her side, but the middle-aged lady was intent on the Chariot Race.

"Look, aunt Bryan ; do see this little boy ! "

" The *chiar-oscuro*, my dear," murmured aunt Bryan, drawing her head back and turning it one side while pursing up her eyes.

Remus noticed the young lady in one of his inter-

vals of taking breath between his long pulls at the
picture. She was the whitest blonde imaginable;
her hair the glinting kind which seems to sparkle as
the head is turned; her lips and cheeks blooming;
her dress was elegant, with a dash of girlish coquetry
in it. She was beyond doubt a child of the wealth-
iest class. She was a surprise to him, like the Chariot
Race itself. Allie was pretty, but this young lady
was wonderful. He looked at her with shy delight.
She smiled and offered him her opera-glass. He
took it and thanked her, and then his ingenuous little
face grew red.

"How do you fix it?" said he.

She showed him how to fix it. He thanked her
again and held it carefully before Rome's nose. And
after Rome had performed the delightful feat of
staring through an opera-glass he gave Arty's big
optics a chance. Last of all he took a quick glimmer
himself, saw the black-browed charioteer and his
galloping horses start out even more distinctly on the
canvas, and the driver on the inside track grinning
through closed teeth, the excited Roman populace
and the soul-stirring confusion; then he gave back
the glass with a little bob of his head and another
"thank you."

"Little *pater familias*," said the young lady in the

lowest but clearest of voices, laughing charmingly at him ; "are these your brother and sister?"

"Yes, ma'am."

JIPPETY.

"Did you notice, aunt Bryan, he brought the little girl in on his arm?"

"He paid our way, too," added Maude, proudly.

"He did! he's a nice brother, isn't he?"

"He's the nicest of everybody."

They all turned to the picture again, but the young lady kept her side regards on him, still smiling, though half sad. She had one of those faces on which every emotion was pictured; and when Rheem looked at her again, which he could not help doing, for she was fascinating, she said to her companion:

"Now see, aunt Bryan, can't you see some resemblance to Marty?"

"Ah!" said aunt Bryan, turning, and rustling all over — she was portly and her dress very stiff — "the little boy? yes, a bright eye — healthy little boy."

Aunt Bryan took her glass and rustled to another picture at the side of the room; not to examine it, but to chat in an undertone with an acquaintance.

The young lady put her glove on Rheem's little fist. "Do you know who I am?" she said in a childish way — she was just out of boarding-school and her young-lady airs set lightly on her yet — "I am Miss Jippety Dalrymple, and I once had a little brother like you."

Remus did not know what else to say, so he bobbed his head again and said to her, all so bashfully:

"How do you do?"

"'How do you do!' hear the little fellow; you dear pretty boy! How old are you?"

"Nine," and he added modestly, feeling that his

card was called for, "my name's Rheem Dogberry."

" Marty would have been nine."

"What's become of him, ma'am ? "

"Dead." Miss Jippety swallowed with a little gasp, and the tears rushed to her eyes. "A little fellow in pants and kilts ; always called me Jippety — my name's Jasper — he's gone — I never can have my brother again — oh ! the little darling ! the little darling ! " Her fair face filled with blood ; she bit her lip hard.

Rome and Remus looked piteously at each other.

"I never can get over it," said Miss Jippety, regaining self-control. "I rather have him with me than to have everything else I want. If I had a little brother like you I should be the happiest girl in the world."

Rome linked her arm in Remus's, as if to prevent Miss Jippety from kidnapping him.

He considered ; he did not know what to say to comfort her. A bright idea struck him :

"Our house burnt down. I'd hated it awfully if any of the children had been burnt up. As it was, Jack's eyes were burnt."

Miss Jippety wiped her eyes and tried to smile again. "Ah ! Is Jack your brother ? I'm sorry he is hurt."

"Yes, ma'am. I have three brothers and three sisters."

"Seven! What a gay family you must be!"

"Yes, ma'am; we always had pretty good times."

"And do you play papa to all of them?"

"Oh, no; they're nearly all older than I am. Ben plays the papa."

"Why, haven't you father and mother?"

"No, 'm."

"Neither have I."

"We got along very well, though," continued Remus, who now felt very confidential towards Miss Jippety, "till our lots were taken away from us and our house caught fire and burned down just when we'd put an addition to it, and raised the kitchen and all!"

"Why, who took your lots? where were they?"

"In New Town. And I think it was a minor heir, Mr. McKay said, that took them and put up an elevator on one of them."

"*What* minor heir?" asked Jippety, opening her eyes.

"It was a minor heir that had the best title," put in Rome, "our father paid money for the land, but the other folks had the best title; and we can't ever, ever get it back unless the other folks give us a — what is that we put in our letter to Joslyn, Rheemie?"

"A quit-claim."

" Yes, a quit-claim."

The murmur of their voices disturbed several people in the room, who turned their heads to look at the group of children and the young lady. She sat in silence with her brows puckered, and seemed to be thinking.

"They built an elevator on your lots, did they?" she whispered again presently. "What is the name of the minor heir who took them from you?"

"I don't know," whispered back Remus; "I heard but I forget."

"And where are the lots? In New Town?—this State?"

"Yes, ma'am."

"And your name is—it seems as if it must be Marty, your face is so like his."

"My name's Rheem Dogberry, and my sister's name's Maude, and my little brother's is Arthur. We lost *him* once. He ran off and got hurt."

"I didn't like it at all," said Arthur solemnly.

"And what did you do after you lost your house?" pursued Miss Jippety, returning to the subject of the lots; "did you have plenty of property besides?"

"Oh, *no*, ma'am; we hadn't anything, except four hundred dollars that belonged to Rome and me, and Jack's hundred. But the rest wouldn't use that. So

we came up here to Chicago and got rooms and went
to work."

"Bless it! how mannish it is," said Jippety, patting his smooth temple. "Are you going to stay here
awhile longer?"

"Till Rome and Arty get tired of looking at the
Chariot Race. *I* never get tired of it."

He fell to enjoying it once more, as Miss Jippety,
keeping her eye still on the children, crossed the
room and murmured with her aunt.

"Jasper, my dear," said aunt Bryan, speaking
nearly aloud, "what freak have you taken?"

"His face is like Marty's, aunt. And it must be
the very same elevator uncle was telling us about.
And they had nothing except those lots."

"But your uncle is a man of business, and he knows
what is right."

"Their father paid for them, and it seems so cruel
they should be obliged to give up their own for a
mere flaw in papers."

"Now, Jasper, my dear, you don't know anything
at all about it. Consult with your uncle when you go
home, and don't let your impulses run away with you."

"I shall be eighteen in a month, aunt, and then
I'm going to give those children a quit-claim for their

lots. *I* dont want their lots. What do I care for a trumpery grain-elevator!"

"I presume your uncle will care if he has invested money for you in it. But there! do, child, control your impulses."

"I will, aunt; I'll tell them I'll clear their title, so my word will be pledged, and I sha'n't have any impulse to forget it."

She went to Remus and put her hands on his shoulders: "My name is Jippety Dalrymple. I didn't know about your land before, but I presume *I* am the minor heir, for whom it has been claimed. I shall be eighteen in a month, however, and then I'll give you that quit-claim — or whatever it is — so your family will get their own again. Won't you kiss me for my little brother Marty's sake?"

Remus flushed to his scalp, but he put his arms and lips up and kissed her heartily.

"Ah, what a nice little brother you are!"

"But how much must we pay?" cried he, eagerly.

"Nothing — nothing — it shall all be fixed up comfortably."

"But we want to do the fair thing!" urged Reemie, in a tremble of delight. "I never had any notion *you* was a minor heir."

Miss Jippety laughed her pretty laugh again. She

shook hands with Maude and also with Arty; but she was a partial little lady, and gave Remus nearly her entire regards.

"Well you shall do the fair thing — *you* always *would* do the the fair thing, Marty —" and with one last little pat she rustled off beside her aunt.

"O Rome!" said Remus.

"O Rheem!" said Rome.

Then they both said, "O Arty!" and Arty said, "O, what!"

"Why, that lady's going to give us our lots back! My gracious, won't the rest of 'em be glad!"

Miss Jippety came back, more beautiful still for being in a hurry, and therefore more vivid in eyes and lips, and said, bending over the back of the seat:

"Will you give me your street and number?"

"Yes 'm;" exclaimed Remus, eagerly, "come and see us, do!" She smiled at his hearty country ways as she made a memorandum of his address.

CHAPTER XXI.

LIGHT AT LAST.

"YES?" said Miss Gaff when Rome and Rheem and Arty rushed in upon her and Alice with this news. "But don't count on it too much."

"She *said* she could do it, Miss Gaff! We never knew it was the minor heir!"

"Those children are always tumbling into good fortune," said Allie.

"Oh, yes," said Miss Gaff. "She gushed. It's easy enough to gush, but people change their minds, and there are her aunt and uncle who will probably influence her against giving up what she might keep. It's a selfish world!"

"*You* aren't selfish, Miss Gaff."

"*Me?* yes, I am — selfish as I can be."

"But you're lovely to us."

"That's because I like you. If I didn't like

you I'd shovel you out of the house in no time!"

"I like selfish people," said Rheem.

It was several weeks afterwards that Loo in her kitchen was compounding a lovely soup for dinner. Ben could not come home in the middle of the day, so their meals up-stairs had gradually settled into breakfast, lunch at noon, and dinner at six o'clock. By that time all the Bunch clustered in. Jack was there the greater part of the day to be sure: but even Jack took his outings with his head tied up. Loo walked him down-stairs, and up and down various streets. Jack and Loo were more united than formerly. Of course Arty always walked at his right hand and chatted about everything. But Jack's tall sister was very companionable, very sweet. Her arm through his was gentle; her voice had pretty cadences in it. Jack felt how womanly she was and remarked:

"Loo, I bet you're getting better looking than Sweet Alice."

Loo laughed: a ripple laugh like the undulations of her figure.

"I don't see," said Jack, "how you can do so much work and take such care of the whole tribe and have time to get pretty. I thought the pretty girls were the ones that kept fussing with themselves all the time."

"It's well you're bandaged Jack, or you wouldn't admire me so much."

"I wish I could take these bands off and try to see — believe I *could* use my eyes a little!"

"Don't do it for the world!" exhorted Lucy, and from that time she watched him very narrowly. If his impatient hands even went to his head, Loo thought of some funny thing to tell him which instantly diverted his mind from sight to hearing.

It was now November weather, sharp and clear. Loo could see the lake tossing and masts rocking, as she made up her soup. Jack and Arty had followed her into the kitchen, Jack on a camp-chair which Ben made for him, and Arty so close he might almost be said to be upon Jack's elbow. Jack felt the knife with which she chipped the vegetables, the smooth top of the table, the long, sleeved, pocketed, tied-back calico apron in which Loo worked, and which she hung in the kitchen closet when she came to the head of the table in her neat alpaca.

"Lucy, do you ever get tired?"

"Of course I do, Jack-straws."

"What puzzles one is how you can keep everything going so, and plan and manage as Ben says you can, and not wear out! Do you love to keep house?"

"I think I do," said Loo; "I love to see everything in order and everybody comfortable. A spoilt
dish or an ugly room just hurts me. Why, I believe
I could keep twice as many rooms as ours, but one
has to think ahead. I know what we're going to
have for dinner next Friday, and I have my break-
fasts planned for all next week."

"I tell you what," cried Jack, "if you get your
deserts you'll marry a nabob with a big house and
everything nice in it, and then you'll entertain people royally, and I'll have a standing invitation; but
won't you hate to have a poor old blind man sitting
in the corner, with a shingle pinned in front of him
saying, ' Please pity the afflicted?' "

"Not at all," laughed Loo; "for if I marry such
an old fellow it's likely *he* will have the rheumatism
or be a chronic invalid, and I can nurse you both
together!"

The door opened from the vestibule and somebody came in saying:

"Who's this I hear talking about being an old
blind man?"

Jack jumped up. "That's cousin Joslyn; I know
his voice!"

Joslyn took his hands, and then dropped them and

shook him by the shoulders and then patted him on the head, then he kissed one of the long slim hands Loo had just wiped nice and clean to give him, and tossed Arty up, exclaiming, " Hullo, Metempsychosis ! "

Before Allie, who piloted him up, shut the door, Ben came bounding up-stairs, and the twins' voices were heard resounding on a lower flight.

Thus Joslyn was surrounded by the Bunch ; and Miss Gaff followed to ask them all down to dine with her. Joslyn pleased her. But as Loo had dinner prepared and was ready to spread her table, she demurred, so Miss Gaff was kept to dine with the Bunch. They all got around Joslyn and looked at him with the hearty affection he appreciated so much. He was handsomer, a very little thinner, but rich colored, magnetic, cordial as ever. They inquired about his mother, and about Mrs. Wylie's last illness. He told them how she had been taken from one place to another, and how she died quietly with his hand in hers. He mentioned in connection with her death, how fond she was of Allie, and that she had mentioned Allie in her will, leaving her a little legacy of a couple of thousand dollars.

The children turned and stared at each other. A couple of thousand dollars ! It seemed **very** little to

Joslyn, but to them it seemed immense. Ben shook hands with her, and the rest of the Bunch solemnly followed his example.

"You are the quaintest lot!" said Joslyn laughing. "Now how much are you going to put into the Association fund, Allie?"

"I ought to put in a great deal," said she sincerely; "for we have had no surplus to start a fund since we were burnt out."

"Come into the parlor, do," begged Lucy, "you're crowding my range so I can't lift my kettle lids, and you'll be steamed full of dinner before I can serve it up."

"Yes, come," cried Joslyn, "for I have something to show Jack there." He put his arm across Jack's shoulder and drew him along. Allie went ahead and let down the shades and made the room as dark as possible.

"I guess you forget, cousin, that I'm the organman — where's my monkey? — yes, here's Arty — here's my monkey — good people have pity on the blind!"

"And here's your organ," laughed Joslyn, dropping on one knee and giving Jack one arm to turn. With the most comical effect in the world, he made a creaking in his throat and began to rhyme and sing in a melancholy key. The whole spontaneous performance was so like Joslyn that the Bunch applauded with ecstacy:

" Ki-wee, ki-wow, I've tramped to-day
Till my old back with dust is gray,
My crank goes round, my one leg quakes:
Oh how an old hand-organ aches!

" Ki-wee, ki-wow ;—ki-wow, ki-wee!
Have you a cent you'll give to me?
Click!—caught my breath —sweet Spirit hear
My prayer, for I'm tormented here!

" Ki-wee, ki-wow, I wander round,
The saddest thing above the ground.
No monkey trick amuses me.
If you'll not pay I'll quit—Ki-wee-e ! "

" Jack, my good fellow," said Joslyn leaping up and forcing Jack into a chair, " your interesting family are now around you ; you have been in darkness some months. The doctor decided at last to let you have your bandages off — providing you return to broad daylight slowly — and as Allie said they were to loose you from bondage this evening, I begged the privilege of being the party to do it. Here you are, sir. Can you look up and see your interesting kinsman ?"

A MOST MOMENTOUS MOMENT.

Jack blinked even in the dark, and caught his breath as the last wrapping fell.

" Well, I'm glad ! " said he. " I *can* see you. I've had some blinks of daylight when the doctor was dressing my eyes, but it hurt me so I could hardly tell whether I saw or not. How'de do Ben ? I have'nt seen you since the fire ! How'de do, Loo — the giantess is going to be the prettiest of the lot, Allie ! "

Jack shook hands on all sides and the girls heartily kissed him. Then he went about the rooms peeping close at things, and followed by two or three of his family who admonished him not to strain his eyes, not attempt any print, and to shield his orbs carefully when he ventured near a window. Arty, who trotted close by as usual, patronized Jack thus :

" Jacky, what's this ? " laying his hand on a broom.

" Oh, a hand-saw," said Jack, good-naturedly.

" No, it isn't ! it's a broom. Now what's this ? "

" The letter O," said Jack.

"No, it isn't ! it's the table."

" This is a pretty good looking place," said Jack, pronouncing on the whole flat. " Oh ! we're going to do glorious things now that there isn't a disabled one among us ! "

" Jack is getting up steam," said Joslyn.

" I've been hissing with it for three months," said Jack, taking in a very long and loud breath.

" Tremendous things will grow out of this house in the air I suppose," said Joslyn.

Loo was laying the table in the dining-room, and Alice and Miss Gaff, with evident enjoyment, were helping her.

Jack had come back from his tour of inspection, and camped on the floor near Joslyn's feet.

" Well, we'll amount to something I think. Ben's going to be an architect. Allie's got such luck in that money she can buy herself a piano and learn music as much as she wants to. Loo's bound to make the most tremendous old housekeeper that ever lived, and I think Rheem will go for printing or something about newspapers, and Rome and Arty will be celebrated for their good looks if for nothing else! *I'm* in for railroading, of course."

" I shouldn' wonder," said Joslyn mischievously, " if I'd tease Allie into coming and living with my mother and me, some day."

" I think that'd be just as mean as mean could be ! " cried Rome with tears in her eyes.

" We couldn't break up the Bunch that way," reasoned Remus, seriously. " Oh, by the way," said

Miss Gaff, coming to the parlor soon, "the postman has left a letter for you, Ben. Did you get it?"

"I have it in my pocket," cried Allie. "I forgot it."

The letter was from Mr. McKay; and when Ben had read it, he said, "Well!" with a light breaking all over his face. "Well, well!"

"She's done it, has she?" said Miss Gaff. "Well, that's better than I expected."

Mr. McKay wrote that the Dalrymple heir, immediately on coming of age had cleared the Dogberry title, and not only were the lots their own now, but the building upon it was theirs.

This well-to-do family broke into joyful exclama tions. One declared their troubles were blessings in masquerade; another shouted that it was splendid; Jack bawled "Le's all go to Europe!" Rheem cried that she was the prettiest and nicest young lady in Chicage or America!—if you only could see her eyes!—and her hair!

"She said Rheem looked just like her little brother Marty," said Rome.

"Let's build a summer residence on the old place!" cried Jack.

"No, no, let's stay here," said Ben, "where we can make our way in the world."

"Better divide into two parties," quizzed Joslyn, "and so cover both fields at once."

The idea of their ever being separated seemed ludicrous; they all laughed at it, except Rome, who thought of Seth Thomas, and Priscilla White's close bedroom, and felt lonesome achings come up in her throat.

I cannot say that they all fell upon each other's necks, but they fell to their dinner, and Joslyn and Miss Gaff exchanged amused looks as their earnest talk went round.

Just there I shall leave them, their paths in life indicated, their hearts all beating as one heart, their hands clustering together; a cosy, warm, ripening Bunch; a Bunch of the truest lovers in the world.

FINIS.

Illustrated Stories for Young Folks.

Young Folks' Cyclopedia of Stories. Quarto, cloth, 3.00.

Contains in one large book the following stories with many illustrations: Five Little Peppers, Two Young Homesteaders, Royal Lowrie's Last Year at St. Olaves, The Dogberry Bunch, Young Rick, Nan the New-Fashioned Girl, Good-for-Nothing Polly and The Cooking Club of Tu-Whit Hollow.

What the Seven Did ; or, the Doings of the Wordsworth Club. By Margaret Sidney. Quarto, boards, 1.75.

The Seven are little girl neighbors who meet once a week at their several homes. They helped others and improved themselves.

Me and My Dolls. By L. T. Meade. Quarto, 50 cts.

A family history. Some of the dolls have had queer adventures. Twelve full-page illustrations by Margaret Johnson.

Little Wanderers in Bo-Peep's World. Quarto, boards, double lithograph covers, 50 cts.

Polly and the Children. By Margaret Sidney. Boards, quarto, 50 cts.

The story of a funny parrot and two charming children. The parrot has surprising adventures at the children's party and wears a medal after the fire.

Five Little Peppers. By Margaret Sidney. 12mo, 1.50.

Story of five little children of a fond, faithful and capable "mamsie." Full of young life and family talk.

Seal Series. 10 vols., boards, double lithographed covers, quarto.

Rocky Fork, Old Caravan Days, The Dogberry Bunch, by Mary H. Catherwood; The Story of Honor Bright and Royal Lowrie's Last Year at St. Olaves, by Charles R. Talbot; Their Club and Ours, by John Preston True; From the Hudson to the Neva, by David Ker; The Silver City, by Fred A. Ober; Two Young Homesteaders, by Theodora Jenness; The Cooking Club of Tu-whit Hollow, by Ella Farman.

Cats' Arabian Nights. By Abby Morton Diaz. Quarto, cloth, 1.75 ; boards, 1.25.

The wonderful cat story of cat stories told by Pussyanita that saved the lives of all the cats.

Young Folks' Illustrated Quartos.

Wide Awake Volume Z. Quarto, boards, 1.75.
Good literature and art have been put into this volume. Henry Bacon's paper about Rosa Bonheur, the great painter of horses and lions, and Steffeck's painting of Queen Louise with Kaiser William would do credit to any Art publication.

Chit Chat for Boys and Girls. Quarto, boards, 75 cts.
A volume of selected pieces upon every conceivable subject. As a distinctive feature it devotes considerable space to Home Life and Sports and Pastimes.

Good Cheer for Boys and Girls.
Short stories, sketches, poems, bits of history, biography and natural history.

Our Little Men and Women for 1888. Quarto, boards, 1.50.
No boys and girls who have this book can be ignorant beyond their years of history, natural history, foreign sights or the good times of other boys and girls.

Babyland for 1888. Quarto, boards, 75 cts.
Finger-plays, cricket stories, Tales told by a Cat and scores of jingles and pictures. Large print and easy words. Colored frontispiece.

Kings and Queens at Home. By Frances A. Humphrey. Quarto, boards, 50 cts.
Short-story accounts of living royal personages.

Queen Victoria at Home. By Frances A. Humphrey. Quarto, boards, 50 cts.
Pen picture of a noble woman. It will aid in educating the heart by presenting the domestic side of the queen's character.

Stories about Favorite Authors. By Frances A. Humphrey. Quarto, boards, 50 cts.
Little literature lessons for little boys and girls.

Child Lore. Edited by Clara Doty Bates. Quarto, cloth, tinted edges, 2.25; boards, 1.50.
More than 50,000 copies sold. The most successful quarto for children.

Helpful Books for Young Folks

Danger Signals. By Rev. F. E. Clark, President of the United Society of Christian Endeavor. 12mo, cloth, 75 cts.
The enemies of youth from the business man's standpoint. The substance of a series of addresses delivered two or three years ago in one of the Boston churches.

Marion Harland's Cookery for Beginners. 12mo, vellum cloth, 75 cts.
The untrained housekeeper needs such directions as will not confuse and discourage her. Marion Harland makes her book simple and practical enough to meet this demand.

Bible Stories. By Laurie Loring. 4to, boards, 35 cts.
Very short stories with pictures. The Creation, Noah and the Dove, Samuel, Joseph, Elijah, the Christ Child, the Good Shepherd, Peter, etc.

The Magic Pear. Oblong, 8vo, boards, 75 cts.
Twelve outline drawing lessons with directions for the amusement of little folks. They are genuine pencil puzzles for untaught fingers. A pear gives shape to a dozen animal pictures.

What O'Clock Jingles. By Margaret Johnson. Oblong, 8vo, boards, 75 cts.
Twelve little counting lessons. Pretty rhymes for small children. Twenty-seven artistic illustrations by the author.

Ways for Boys to Make and Do Things. 60 cts.
Eight papers by as many different authors, on subjects that interest boys. A book to delight active boys and to inspire lazy ones.

Our Young Folks at Home. 4to, boards, 1.00.
A collection of illustrated prose stories by American authors and artists. It is sure to make friends among children of all ages. Colored frontispiece.

Peep of Day Series. 3 vols., 1.20 each.
Peep of Day, Line upon Line, Precept upon Precept. Sermonettes for the children, so cleverly preached that the children will not grow sleepy.

Home Primer. Boards, square, 8vo, 50 cts.
A book for the little ones to learn to read in before they are old enough to be sent off to school. 100 illustrations.

Natural History.

Stories and Pictures of Wild Animals. By Anna F. Burnham. Quarto, boards, 75 cts.

Big letters, big pictures and easy stories of elephants, lions, tigers, lynxes, jaguars, bears and many others.

Life and Habits of Wild Animals. Quarto, cloth, 1.50.

The very best book young folks can have if they are at all interested in Natural History. If they are not yet interested it will make them so. Illustrated from designs by Joseph Wolf.

Children's Out-Door Neighbors. By Mrs. A. E. Andersen-Maskell. 3 volumes, 12mo, cloth, each 1.00.

Three instructive and interesting books: Children with Animals, Children with Birds, Children with Fishes. The author has the happy faculty of interesting boys and girls in the wonderful neighbors around them and that without introducing anything which is not borne out by the knowledge of learned men.

Some Animal Pets. By Mrs. Oliver Howard. Quarto, boards, 35 cts.

The experiences of a Colorado family with young, wild and tame animals. It is one of the pleasantest animal books we have met in many a day. Well thought, well written, well pictured, the book itself, apart from its contents, is attractive. Full page pictures.

Tiny Folk in Red and Black. Quarto, boards, 35 cts.

The tiny folk are ants and they make as interesting a study as human folk — perhaps more interesting in the opinion of some. The book gives a full and graphic description of their many wise and curious ways — how they work, how they harvest their grain, how they milk their cows, etc. It will teach the children to keep eyes and ears open.

My Land and Water Friends. By Mary E. Bamford. Seventy illustrations by Bridgman. Quarto, cloth, 1.50.

The frog opens the book with a "talk" about himself, in the course of which he tells us all about the changes through which he passes before he arrives at perfect froghood. Then the grasshopper talks and is followed by others, each giving his view of life from his own individual standpoint.

ABOUT GIANTS. By Isabel Smithson. Boston:
D. Lothrop Company. Price 60 cents. In this
little volume Miss Smithson has gathered together
many curious and interesting facts relating to
real giants, or people who have grown to an ex-
traordinary size. She does not believe that there
was ever a race of giants, but that those who are
so-called are exceptional cases, due to some freak
of nature. Among those described are Cutter,
the Irish giant, who was eight feet tall, Tony
Payne, whose height exceeded seven feet, and
Chang, the Chinese giant, who was on exhibition
in this country a few years ago. The volume
contains not only accounts of giants, but also of
dwarfs, and is illustrated.

AMERICAN AUTHORS. By Amanda B. Harris.
Boston: D. Lothrop Company. Price $1.00. This
is one of the books we can heartily commend to
young readers, not only for its interest, but for
the information it contains. All lovers of books
have a natural curiosity to know something about
their writers, and the better the books, the keener
the curiosity. Miss Harris has written the various
chapters of the volume with a full appreciation of
this fact. She tells us about the earlier group of
American writers, Irving, Cooper, Prescott, Emer-
son, and Hawthorne, all of whom are gone, and
also of some of those who came later, among
them the Cary sisters, Thoreau, Lowell, Helen
Hunt, Donald G. Mitchell and others. Miss Harris has a happy way of imparting information, and
the boys and girls into whose hands this little
book may fall will find it pleasant reading.

THE ART OF LIVING. From the Writings of Samuel Smiles. With Introduction by the venerable Dr. Peabody of Harvard University, and Biographical Sketch by the editor, Carrie Adelaide Cooke. Boston : D. Lothrop Company. Price $1.00.

Samuel Smiles is the Benjamin Franklin of England. His sayings have a similar terseness, aptness and force; they are directed to practical ends, like Franklin s; they have the advantage of being nearer our time and therefore more directly related to subjects upon which practical wisdom is of practical use

Success in life is his subject all through, The Art of Living; and he confesses on the very first page that "happiness consists in the enjoyment of little pleasures scattered along the common path of life, which in the eager search for some great and exciting joy we are apt to overlook. It finds delight in the performance of common duties faithfully and honorably fulfilled."

Let the reader go back to that quotation again and consider how contrary it is to the spirit that underlies the businesses that are nowadays tempting men to sudden fortune, torturing with disappointments nearly all who yield, and burdening the successful beyond their endurance, shortening lives and making them weary and most of them empty.

Is it worth while to join the mad rush for the lottery; or to take the old road to slow success ?

This book of the chosen thoughts of a rare philosopher leads to contentment as well as wisdom; for, when we choose the less brilliant course because we are sure it is the best one, we have the most complete and lasting repose from anxiety.

MONTEAGLE. By Pansy. Boston: D. Lothrop Company. Price 75 cents. Both girls and boys will find this story of Pansy's pleasant and profitable reading. Dilly West is a character whom the first will find it an excellent thing to intimate, and boys will find in Hart Hammond a noble, manly, fellow who walks for a time dangerously near temptation, but escapes through providential influences, not the least of which is the steady devotion to duty of the young girl, who becomes an unconscious power of good.

A DOZEN OF THEM. By Pansy. Boston: D. Lothrop Company. Price 60 cents. A Sunday-school story, written in Pansy's best vein, and having for its hero a twelve-year-old boy who has been thrown upon the world by the death of his parents, and who has no one left to look after him but a sister a little older, whose time is fully occupied in the milliner's shop where she is employed. Joe, for that is the boy's name, finds a place to work at a farmhouse where there is a small private school. His sister makes him promise to learn by heart a verse of Scripture every month. It is a task at first, but he is a boy of his word, and he fulfills his promise, with what results the reader of the story will find out. It is an excellent book for the Sunday-school.

AT HOME AND ABROAD. Stories from *The Pansy* Boston: D. Lothrop Company. Price, $1.00. A score of short stories which originally appeared in the delightful magazine, *The Pansy*, have been here brought together in collected form with the illustrations which originally accompanied them. They are from the pens of various authors, and are bright, instructive and entertaining

TILTING AT WINDMILLS : A Story of the Blue Grass Country. By Emma M. Connelly. Boston: D. Lothrop Company. 12mo, $1.50.

NOT since the days of " A Fool's Errand " has so strong and so characteristic a " border novel " been brought to the attention of the public as is now presented by Miss Connelly in this book which she so aptly terms "Tilting at Windmills." Indeed, it is questionable whether Judge Tourgee's famous book touched so deftly and yet so practically the real phases of the reconstruction period and the interminable antagonisms of race and section.

The self-sufficient Boston man, a capital fellow at heart, but tinged with the traditions and environments of his Puritan ancestry and conditions, coming into his strange heritage in Kentucky at the close of the civil war, seeks to change by instant manipulation all the equally strong and deep-rooted traditions and environments of Blue Grass society.

His ruthless conscience will allow of no compromise, and the people whom he seeks to proselyte alike misunderstand his motives and spurn his proffered assistance.

Presumed errors are materialized and partial evils are magnified. Allerton tilts at windmills and with the customary Quixotic results. He is, seemingly, unhorsed in every encounter.

Miss Connelly's work in this, her first novel, will make readers anxious to hear from her again and it will certainly create, both in her own and other States, a strong desire to see her next forthcoming work announced by the same publishers in one of their new series—her " Story of the State of Kentucky."